He'd meant to talk to Cate before now.

At least phone her. But each time he'd made the decision he'd backtracked. How did you solve the insoluble?

By Thursday Cate was going crazy.

She couldn't believe he'd made no effort to see her outside of the surgery, but there had been nothing from him. Nothing to reinforce the fact that, physically, they'd been as close as any two people could have been. They'd become lovers, for heaven's sake. As she made her way to his consulting room she was left with the stark, miserable conclusion that he'd been merely using her.

Yet somehow, deep within her, she couldn't believe that. Wouldn't.

Leah Martyn's writing career began at age eleven, when she wrote the winning essay in the schoolwork section of a country show. As an adult, success with short stories led her to try her hand at a longer work. With her daughter training to become a Registered Nurse, the highs and lows of hospital life touched a chord, and writing Medical Romances™ liberally spiked with humour became a reality. Home is with her husband in semi-rural Queensland. Her hobbies include an involvement with live theatre and relaxing on the beach with a good book.

Recent titles by the same author:

FOR PERSONAL REASONS
ALWAYS MY VALENTINE

THE LOVING FACTOR

BY
LEAH MARTYN

MILLS & BOON®

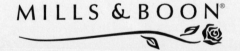

First published in Great Britain 2001
Large Print edition 2001
Harlequin Mills & Boon Limited,
Eton House, 18-24 Paradise Road,
Richmond, Surrey TW9 1SR

© Leah Martyn 2001

ISBN 0 263 16847 6

Set in Times Roman 17 on 19 pt.
17-0701-37759

Printed and bound in Great Britain
by Antony Rowe Ltd, Chippenham, Wiltshire

CHAPTER ONE

CATE was glad she'd done it.

Last night she'd finally found the will to gather up Rick's paraphernalia, stuff he'd obviously been uninterested in retrieving from her flat. She'd bundled everything into a giant-sized bin bag and now she was about to donate it to her local charity shop.

Her mouth curled into a rueful little moue. Their engagement had been brief and now, eight months on and with the benefit of hindsight, Cate wondered how she and Rick De Lisle had ever thought they'd had the makings of a marriage.

She saw their relationship clearly now, felt a chill run up her spine at what might have happened.

But it hadn't. And giving herself no more time to reconstruct the past, she hitched up the bag with its tangible reminders and swung purposefully out of her car.

Several minutes later, mission accomplished, Cate was back in her Volkswagen Polo and heading towards Ferndale Medical Centre where she was employed as a general practitioner.

The group practice was situated in one of Brisbane's older built-up suburbs and Cate was glad she'd made the move to the smaller practice. She'd been there for six months, the third doctor in a team of three.

The others were male. Peter Maguire, in his mid-fifties, was the founding partner and Jon Goodsir was just completing his second year with Ferndale.

They were a good bunch at the practice, Cate thought, battling her way through stop-start early morning traffic. Ten minutes later she was pulling into the rear car park of the stone-washed, single-storey building.

Lifting her medical bag from the passenger seat, she alighted from the car and stood for a moment, breathing in the cool crispness of an August morning.

Yet already the air seemed to hold the foretaste of summer, the promise of long, warm days to come. What would this summer bring?. Cate wondered, her thoughts oddly unsettled as she made her way past the bank of wildly flowering shrubs to the rear entrance.

In her surgery Cate shrugged out of her jacket, and began to sift through the mail Chrissie Jones, the receptionist, had left on her desk. With relief she drew out the envelope containing the X-rays she'd been waiting for. She stood and with a few deft movements placed the first of the films on the viewing screen.

'Oh, Cate. Good, you're in.' Chrissie popped her fair head around the door. 'Could you see an early bird?'

Damn. Cate glanced at her watch. So much for trying to get a jump-start this morning. 'Who is it, Chrissie?'

'Lauren Bentley.'

Cate's brown eyes widened speculatively. It was only days since she'd done Lauren's six-week postnatal check. 'If it's urgent, I'd better see her.'

The receptionist made a small face. 'I don't think it's medically urgent. Apparently she's had an offer of work. Wants to check with you about the baby's welfare before she commits.'

Cate's smile was wry. 'In that case, better trot her along, then. I'll have a word.'

'Thanks, Cate.' Chrissie withdrew her head and then popped it back. 'Join us for coffee when you're through?'

'Lovely.' Cate shoved her bag out of sight under the desk. 'By the way, who's in and who's out?'

'Jon's doing hospital and home visits and Peter's gracing the golf course.' Chrissie grinned. 'In about nine-thirty, he said. And Dr Whittaker's here.'

'I understood he was due to start next week.' Involuntarily, Cate touched the silver chain at her throat. 'Does he want the tour?'

'Didn't say.' Chrissie arched an eyebrow. 'Are you ready for Lauren now?'

'Two minutes.' Cate stifled a sigh, settling her long-line black sweater over her hips, seeing her squirrelled-away time block vanish like leaves in the wind.

Now it seemed she was going to have to be the one to show Andrew Whittaker around. Damn and blast. The least Peter could have done was to be here. The man was his nephew after all, covering for Peter while the senior doctor took an extended holiday.

Oh, well, it was pointless getting wound up about it. Cate sank into her chair, just succeeding in bringing up Lauren Bentley's details on the screen when her patient walked in.

'Thanks for seeing me.' Lauren sat neatly in the chair beside Cate's desk. 'I've been offered part-time work,' she explained. 'I've got an interview with the school principal this morning.'

Cate's hands interlinked in her lap. 'How do you feel about juggling work and motherhood?'

'Well, this work thing's happened a bit earlier than I would have liked.'

'And it's not a perfect world, is it?' Cate smiled.

'No.' Lauren bit her lip. 'The thing is, I really can't afford to knock it back. David and I have a mortgage a horse couldn't jump over.'

'Have you arranged suitable care for your baby?' Cate read through Lauren's notes quickly. She'd had a straightforward delivery and she and her son had checked out well on their postnatal visit.

'My mum's going to take him.' She swallowed. 'But one part of me feels like I'm abandoning him—'

'Don't feel like that, Lauren.' Cate was swift to reassure the young mother. 'You could always express your milk and store it so your mother could bottle-feed young Scott.'

'I was hoping you'd say that.' Lauren's expression cleared. 'I'd hate to wean him. So...' She leant closer to Cate. 'Could I freeze my milk? And could Mum just re-heat it in the microwave?'

'Yes to the first. No to the second,' Cate said. 'Microwaves tend to heat unevenly and it's a fair possibility that some com-ponents in breast milk can be damaged in the process. Like the white blood cells.'

'I had no idea.' Lauren shook her head. 'There's so much to think about.'

'Don't let it become a problem,' Cate said. 'And, look, it's not too difficult once you get the S. and T. method down pat.'

Lauren looked confused.

'The storing and thawing of your milk,' Cate explained. 'And how it can all be done safely. Why don't I jot down some clear guidelines for you?' Cate pulled a scribble block towards her. 'I'm sure I've some relevant information from the Nursing Mothers' Association as well. Perhaps if I pop everything in an envelope and leave it with Chrissie at the front desk, you could pick it up after your interview.'

'Wonderful.' Lauren got to her feet. 'I'm really grateful for your help, Dr Clifford.'

'Any time.' Cate's smile was infectious. 'Remember, I'm just doing what I'm trained to do. The same way you're about to.'

Lauren's mouth tipped into a wry smile. 'Except I'm juggling three jobs now, aren't I? As well as teaching, I have to be Scott's mother and David's wife. But hey!' She gave a cracked laugh. 'I'm an optimist.'

Cate saw her patient out and, leaving the door ajar, turned to focus on the X-ray once more.

'Good morning.'

Cate's head came up quickly so that her cloud of silver-blond hair slid back from her cheekbones. Her gaze stayed riveted on the doorway and on the six-foot-plus male who stood there.

'Hi...' Her breath lodged and then came out slowly. 'Dr Whittaker?'

'Andrew.' The man in question shrugged lazily away from the doorframe and moved across the carpeted space towards her. 'And you're Cate Clifford?' A smile, slow, faintly teasing, played around his lips.

She nodded, feeling the warm firmness of his skin as they shook hands briefly.

'I've been commissioned to tell you coffee's up and to twist your arm if necessary.' He grinned, propping his hip on the edge of her desk. One dark eyebrow rose. 'Does that mean you're some kind of workaholic, Dr Clifford?'

'No more than anyone else has to be in a small practice,' she defended herself. 'We weren't expecting you until next week—' Cate's words came to an abrupt halt as she realised belatedly that they'd sounded like an accusation of some kind.

Oh, Lord, she was overreacting. Cate knew that nothing had prepared her for the sheer *presence* of the man.

Why couldn't he have been small? she fretted, running a swift inventory over his face, tanned, weathered from the outdoors. Married would have been even better. Put him right out of her orbit. 'Peter will be in about nine-thirty,' she said a bit stiltedly.

'Mmm, I know.' Andrew slid off his perch to peer over her shoulder. 'I'm staying with Pete and Ellie until I get my own place. 'Whose foot?' He gestured towards the skeletal framework thrown up by the X-ray.

Cate took a breath to steady herself. 'Fifty-six-year-old male. He's a butcher. Stands on a cement floor for most of his working day. He complained of tenderness in his right instep.'

'You were thinking perhaps of a spur?' The blue eyes lit enquiringly.

'Well…yes.'

His mouth went firm for a moment. 'Well, clearly it's not a spur from what we can see here. No other bony lesion demonstrated either.' Thoughtfully, he stroked his chin with the pad of his thumb.

'A couple of cysts in the first metatarsal head.' Cate indicated the shaded outline. 'But they shouldn't present a problem.'

'No.' Andrew gave a quick smile, the action cutting interesting grooves into his lean cheeks. 'So, Cate, what treatment will you recommend for your butcher?'

Cate flicked off the light on the screen, conscious her heart was fluttering behind her breastbone. She felt almost stifled by

Andrew Whittaker's nearness, running into speech to cover the fact. 'Physio as a priority to try to get some flexibility back.'

'Perhaps a change in the style of his regular work boots or at least some modification could be an option as well. I struck more than my share of feet problems in the army, I can tell you.'

Army? Cate blinked and then remembered. Peter had mentioned that his nephew had been attached to the Australian Defence Forces as an MO for the past several years. Apparently, he'd taken his discharge quite recently.

Cate gave him a brief smile. 'How will you find working in a suburban practice?'

'Different?'

'I expect you'll cope.'

'Gosh, I hope so.'

Cate coloured, realising belatedly that she was being sent up ever so nicely. Of course he'd cope. In today's world, army task forces were being deployed to all kinds of trouble spots. Andrew Whittaker had probably seen more emergencies than she'd had hot dinners!

'I was referring to the change of pace,' she said defensively.

'I know.' Andrew peeled himself away from the wall, shoving his hands into the back pockets of his jeans. 'I was being a smart alec. Sorry.'

Cate made a small sound in her throat. Andrew being a joker was the least of her problems. Just his presence was enough to send rivulets of awareness seeping through her, sweeping away her tenuous hold on common sense like some kind of flotsam. 'Shall we get this coffee, then?'

'Let's.' His smile turned to a crooked little grin. 'Before they send out a search party for us.'

'I'll show you over the place later, if you like.' Somewhat to her surprise, Cate heard herself make the offer.

'Thanks.' He gave a tiny nod of acknowledgement. 'But I'll lean on Pete for that. Your surgery list probably has you strapped for time anyway.'

Cate sent him a dry look. 'Fridays seem to be like that, everyone tending to check out their various problems before the weekend.'

'Mmm.' He looked thoughtful. 'Peculiar creatures, aren't we? Humans, I mean. Do you live nearby?' He'd changed the subject smoothly.

'Not far.' Cate's shoulder brushed against his upper arm as he stood back to let her enter the staffroom.

Their gazes swivelled and caught, and Andrew's eyes held hers for a long moment before he looked away, leaving her feeling oddly shaken and more confused than ever.

'About time, you two!' Chrissie sprang to her feet and began pouring coffee into the cheerful blue-and-yellow-dotted mugs. 'Andrew, black with one, right?' The receptionist pushed the sugar bowl towards him.

'Spot on,' he said. 'And it smells wonderful. Cate?' Courteously, he proffered the bowl of sugar.

She shook her head. 'No, thanks. I take only milk.'

'Morning, everyone.' Bea Harrison, the practice manager, came into the staffroom, scattering a smile among the assembled company. 'And Dr Whittaker. Hello again. Finding your way around?'

'Absolutely.' He shot Bea a grin. 'Coffee's good, too.'

Bea blinked. 'Oh, right.' She jangled her keys on the bench top. 'Can I interest any of you in coming to our school fête tomorrow?'

'Count me out.' Jessica Royal, the RN for the group, raised her smooth auburn head from the magazine she was reading. 'I've a heavy date. We're going to the coast.'

'And I play hockey on Saturdays, Bea.' Chrissie looked dismayed. 'Didn't you say it's to raise funds for the school orchestra or something?'

Bea nodded. 'Both my sons are involved. There's a trip to Adelaide in the offing. The kids have been asked to play in their festival of arts. It'll be great exposure. But unfortunately it all costs money.'

'I guess I could pop in for an hour or so,' Cate said quietly. 'Jon's doing the weekend calls.'

'Oh, Cate, could you?' Bea's smile extended to beaming proportions. 'Every bit helps. And I just might find a little job for you on my cake stall. You as well, Andrew, if you're not busy?'

He looked startled. 'I—uh—I'm flat-hunting, Bea. Sorry.'

'Fine excuse.' Cate stifled a chuckle at his obvious dilemma.

Andrew lifted his mug. 'We'll see,' he murmured, the corners of his eyes crinkling with humour and the merest challenge.

Safely back at her desk a few minutes later, Cate propped her chin on her hand and looked into space. Her breath eased out. A warning light seemed to flash in her head. Keep your feet on the ground, Cate...

With a little sigh she lifted the phone to call her butcher patient, Trevor James. As she dialled the number, her thoughts were still whirling.

She just hoped Andrew Whittaker possessed the nous required for general practice. And if he didn't? Cate shrugged the thought away. They'd just have to try to rub along somehow. After all, it wasn't as though they'd have to be in each other's pockets.

While she waited for Trevor to come to the phone, Cate began riffling through her drawer for some suitable leaflets to give to Lauren Bentley.

And then there was Madeleine Twigg. Cate's mind jumped across to her elderly patient, marooned in her old run-down house with no one to care for her. Or not really. A tiny frown pleated Cate's forehead. She'd have to make time to talk to Peter and Jon about Mrs Twigg. That poor woman needed to be rehoused as a matter of urgency. Although getting her to agree might be another matter.

Cate had barely completed her phone call when there was the sound of a commotion outside. Her head came up, the nerves clenching in the pit of her stomach. They'd already had an attempted robbery at the surgery, an addict demanding drugs. The whole experience had been a nightmare—

'Cate, can you come?' A breathless Chrissie skidded to a halt at Cate's door. 'It's Mr Cameron. He's collapsed!'

Cate sucked in a breath. The prominent MP was Peter's patient. 'What happened?' she demanded as they sped down the corridor to the waiting room.

'He was complaining of indigestion. Asked to see Dr Maguire.' Chrissie bit down on her bottom lip. 'And then his eyes kind of rolled… It was awful…'

'Call an ambulance, Chrissie,' Cate said sharply, her glance sweeping the waiting room and registering that Andrew Whittaker was very definitely in charge. Her lips tightened. This was all they needed—a possible heart attack in the waiting room and the first patients due to arrive any minute.

Jessica also had come running and Cate watched as the RN swiftly disposed of Mr Cameron's tie and in one sweeping movement popped open the buttons on the MP's pristine white shirt.

Andrew was searching for a pulse, his face grim. 'Nothing,' he said shortly. 'We'll need the Oxyviva, please. And the defib. Stat!'

Jessica flew.

Cate's gut clenched. In a flash her training took over. She dropped beside Bart Cameron and began CPR. Heart attacks came like thieves in the night. Cate considered the sober thought, counting the rhythmic beats of resuscitation in her head. They struck without warning, chose their victims at random…

'Keep it going, Cate.' She heard the urgency in Andrew's voice, felt his fingers hard and warm on her shoulder. 'I'll get a line in. And, Chrissie!' He arched back, his gaze intense. 'This isn't a floor show! Lock the doors and keep the patients elsewhere for a bit.' He swung back to Cate. 'Any pulse?'

'No.'

He swore under his breath. 'Let's defib, then. This guy some bigwig?' he snapped, placing the pads on the man's chest.

'Member of Parliament.' Cate's mouth drew in.

'Figures.' A muscle worked briefly in Andrew's jaw. He switched the life-saving machine on.

Cate felt the beat of silence almost tangibly while the machine charged.

'Clear!' Andrew's deep voice shot through the stillness as he discharged the paddles.

Her lips clamped tightly, Cate felt for a pulse and shook her head.

'Adrenalin!' Andrew barked, and Jessica snapped the prepared dose into his hand.

Please, work, Cate prayed silently as Andrew shot the stimulant home and prepared to defib once more.

'Clear!'

'We have a pulse,' Cate confirmed. 'And spontaneous breathing.'

Andrew's face cleared. 'About flaming time.'

'And here's the ambulance.' Jessica scrambled up and ran to the front doors to let the officers in.

'Where shall we send him?' Andrew leant on the counter in Reception and began to scribble on the card Chrissie had given him.

'The PA hospital.' Cate stood aside as the ambulance trolley was snapped into place and the patient gently lifted.

'Which is?' Andrew's dark head swung up as he asked for clarification.

'Oh, the Princess Alexandra,' Cate supplied. She'd forgotten Andrew Whittaker didn't know the city's main hospitals yet. 'It's the closest and the staff are on the ball. He'll get good care.'

'Tell Pete I've gone with Mr Cameron.' Andrew kept his hand on the patient's shoulder as the trolley was wheeled out. 'I'll check back with him when I have some news.'

'Andrew?' Cate called urgently after him.

'Cate?' He looked back and seemed to study her for a moment, his eyes clear and steady.

She edged him a brief smile. 'Thanks.'

'You, too.' His look seemed to go on and on before he turned, following the ambulance trolley out through the glass outer doors.

Cate took a shaken breath, wheeling and walking quickly back to her consulting room, imagining that searching gaze following her until the hairs on the back of her neck began to prickle.

Striding into her room, she gave vent to a huff of disbelief. Stop right there, she warned her heart in exasperation. Andrew Whittaker is here for a matter of weeks only and he's probably on the prowl, looking for a diversion, a chance to unwind after his tour of duty in the army.

She snorted inelegantly. What's the matter with you, Cate? Do you have some kind of addiction to unsuitable men?

Settling into her chair, she steadied herself with several deep breaths, determined to dismiss the silent message in Andrew Whittaker's amazingly blue eyes to the back of her mind.

CHAPTER TWO

AS THE morning wore on, Cate began to feel she was finally getting on top of things. If you didn't count the dreaded paperwork, she decided ruefully.

When her last patient had departed, she began typing her notes into the computer, looking up as the knock sounded on her door.

Chrissie popped her head in. 'I'm off to the deli, Cate. Can I get you anything for lunch?'

'Heavens, is it that time already?' Cate frowned at her watch. 'Better just get sandwiches for everyone, Chrissie.' She pushed back in her chair and stretched. 'I think Peter wants a staff meeting over lunch.'

'Poor you.' The receptionist made a face. 'OK. I'll raid the petty cash.'

'Good idea.' Cate grinned, turning back to her keyboard. Her heart tripped. 'Andrew back yet?'

Chrissie lifted a shoulder. 'Haven't seen him.'

Cate bit down on her bottom lip, not knowing whether to feel regret or relief.

Andrew took his time getting back from the hospital. He had a lot to think about.

OK, it had been a long time—over a year—since he'd had a woman in his life. His life in the army hadn't exactly lent itself to forming, let alone nurturing, a relationship.

But he was done with that now. His spirits lighter, he began to move briskly down the pedestrian walkway to the road, his mind rerunning the events of the morning.

And his meeting with Dr Cate Clifford.

What perfume did she wear? he wondered. He was right out of touch with things like that nowadays. But he could still smell it. A drift of light fragrance still clung to the sleeve of his sweater from when she'd brushed against him.

She was nicely put together, too. Andrew gave free rein to a reminiscent crooked smile. The long jumper and tailored trousers had clung so sweetly to her curves.

Suddenly, and without warning, he felt a stab of want, an ache his body hadn't felt for seemingly aeons.

Hell! He yanked himself up short. Get a grip, Whittaker. But, then, on the other hand…

He began to pick up his pace to a jog, the urge to see her again as sudden and unexpected as a rifle shot.

Cate ran a brush through her hair and added a dash of lipstick, before joining the others in the staffroom for their working lunch.

With quiet efficiency, Bea set out the sandwiches and topped up the coffee-maker in readiness. 'There's boiling water in the kettle if anyone wants tea,' she said.

'I would, Bea. Thanks.' Cate got down a mug and broke open a new packet of tea-bags.

'One for me, too, Cate, while you're there.'

Cate heard Peter's voice, a reassuring rumble, at the door and smiled. 'Coming up. Is Andrew joining us?'

'Mmm, think so. He rang me from the hospital. Bart's holding his own. I guess Andrew will have more details when he gets here.'

'Bit tricky this morning, was it?' Jon Goodsir dumped several files on the table and helped himself to coffee. 'Chrissie was full of it.' He grinned.

Cate lifted a shoulder. 'It could have been worse. We could've had a waiting room full of patients.'

'I've always said Bart had excellent timing.' The senior partner smiled, the action bringing life to his rather tired eyes. Then he sobered. 'But this time I'm going to set him some boundaries and he's going to have to keep them. If not for his own sake, then for Mary's.'

'Probably overweight, is he?' Jon said around a mouthful of salad sandwich. 'Too many high teas in the parliamentary dining room?'

'He's not overly obese.' Peter stirred his tea thoughtfully. 'But the nature of his job rather predetermines his stress factor.'

'And Mr Cameron's in the age bracket for that to be a problem.' Cate was still seeing Bart Cameron's ghastly pallor when the ambulance officers had wheeled him away.

Peter nodded and helped himself to a sandwich. 'I intend handing him over to Andrew anyway.'

'Someone taking my name in vain?' With a leashed kind of energy Andrew bounded into the staffroom. He gave a general greeting, helping himself to coffee and taking the chair next to Cate.

'Found your way back to us, then?' Peter gave his nephew a wry little smile.

'Absolutely.' Andrew spooned sugar into his coffee. 'Well, the cabbie did,' he qualified with a grin. He nodded towards Jon, extending his hand. 'I don't believe we've met. In case you haven't guessed, I'm Andrew Whittaker.'

'Peter did mention you in passing,' the other said drily, his handshake firm. 'Jon Goodsir.'

'Sorry.' Peter flipped a hand in apology. 'My manners must have gone out with the bath water this morning. Jon's our squash champion and third member of our medical team.'

'That's me.' Jon gave a gravelly laugh. 'Age thirty-five, wife Claire, son aged three. Dig in,' he invited, indicating the plate piled with sandwiches.

'I'm fine, thanks,' Andrew refused politely. 'I had something at the hospital canteen.'

Jon chuckled. 'You must've been hungry.'

'I've eaten in worse places,' Andrew said quietly, his blue eyes suddenly without their hint of humour.

'I expect you have.' Cate spoke for the first time. 'Peter told us you were part of the task force sent to assist after that appalling tidal wave in New Guinea recently.'

'Don't make me out a hero, Cate.' His hand thrust dismissively through his dark hair. 'I was only doing my job.'

Cate's look became shuttered. How could he have dismissed her like that? She fought against the sudden hard lump in her chest.

'How are you finding civvy street?' Jon came in with remarkable diplomacy.

'Good,' Andrew said economically, and shot a questioning look at his uncle. 'Do you want the update on Bart Cameron now?'

'Yes, I suppose we'd better.' Peter took his spectacles out of his shirt pocket and slipped them on. 'This is supposed to be a working lunch after all.'

'He's listed as serious but stable.' Andrew wrapped his hands around his coffee-mug. 'It seems it's been a relatively mild MI.'

'The man's been very fortunate, then.' Peter did his own brand of note-taking on Bart Cameron's file.

'I spoke to the attending cardiologist,' Andrew continued. 'They're giving Mr Cameron anti-hypertensive drugs IV and he's on constant ECG to monitor any changes.'

Peter looked at his nephew over the top of his glasses. 'What's the short-term prognosis?'

'Wait and see. Dr Beresford said they'll carry out the usual exercise and stress tests in a couple of days.'

'His last cholesterol levels weren't all that worrisome actually,' Peter said. 'But that's neither here nor there at the moment.'

'His wife arrived before I left the hospital.' Andrew sat back in his chair and locked his hands around the back of his neck. 'Ellie was with her.'

Peter Maguire nodded. 'We've been friends for years. And I know Mary's had worries about Bart's workload. And passed them on to Ellie,' he added a bit ruefully.

'That's probably why she's dragging you away on a long holiday.'

'Probably.' Peter's mouth turned down at the corners. 'And speaking of holidays, we thought of taking off at the end of next week. If that's OK with everyone?' He looked slowly around the table at the medical team.

Cate bit her lip. In reality she hated the thought of Peter leaving, even if it was only temporarily. He was the anchor at Ferndale and, whether the staff realised it or not, they all in some way depended on his quiet wisdom and the gentle way he handled matters.

The thought of Andrew Whittaker replacing him was suddenly leaving Cate feeling very uncertain…

'Don't forget your farewell do is at our place,' Jon reminded him. 'Let us know what night suits you.'

'There's really no need—' Peter's mild protest was howled down immediately. 'Well, OK.' He gave a resigned shrug. 'Thank you all very much. We'll make it Saturday week, then, if that's all right with Claire. Ellie and I are planning to get away on the Sunday. Treating ourselves to a break at the coast before we fly off to Ireland.'

'Hope you won't find any little—uh— surprises over there,' Jon quipped. It was common knowledge that the Maguires were keen to research their respective family trees.

Peter's mouth quirked. 'Ellie seems to think it's quite possible we'll turn up a few black sheep.'

'Only a few?' Andrew gave a laugh. 'What's your opinion, Cate?'

She spun her head to look at him. Found herself staring into his eyes. They had the luminosity of an early morning seascape, she thought fancifully, shakenly. She swallowed. 'About what?'

'Researching family trees.' His dark brows peaked. 'Might be fun to do it together some time.' The flick of a dimple appeared in his cheek as he smiled. 'If you're interested...?'

Cate took a breath and looked quickly away.

'If we could get on to more serious matters?' Jon looked down at the file in front of him. 'I'd like to bring everyone up to date on Shannon Hayward. Her bone-marrow tests indicate acute lymphoblastic leukaemia.'

'Oh, dear.' Peter shook his head. 'That's the family from the housing commission flats in Balmain Street, isn't it?'

'Kurt and Ginny,' Jon confirmed. 'They're real battlers. Do anything for those kids.'

'Mrs Hayward's on my list,' Cate said quietly. 'This news will have hit them very hard.'

'How old is the child?' His blue eyes alert, Andrew looked from one to the other.

'Seven.' Jon rubbed a finger across his forehead. 'There's a sibling, Britt, who's nine.'

Andrew leaned forward earnestly. 'The prognosis for childhood leukaemia is a lot more hopeful these days. Are they receiving counselling?'

'Oh, yes,' Jon said. 'And I've spoken to them, but I honestly don't know if they've managed to take much in. I think it's quite likely they'll have more questions later,' he said consideringly, 'when they start to come to grips with the diagnosis.'

'And if you're not available, you'd like either Cate or me to give them a friendly ear.' Andrew's look held quick perception.

'In a word, yes.' His long arm outstretched, Jon dipped into the tin of digestive biscuits Bea had thoughtfully left. 'It's quite possible that the parents—and grandparents for that matter—will come here to us for some answers.'

Andrew nodded solemnly. 'Consider it done.'

'That goes for me, too,' Cate said, knowing the whole business of sudden hospitalisation and treatment especially for a child could have left the relatives feeling terribly vulnerable.

'Thanks, both of you.' Jon's mouth flattened into a brief smile. 'With Peter gone, we don't want the good name of Ferndale going to the pack. And I'd like to think we could give the Haywards all the support they need.'

'Speaking of support…' Cate leant forward, locking her hands in front of her on the table. 'I'm at my wit's end what to do about Madeleine Twigg.' She turned and met Andrew's eyes fleetingly, explaining, 'My patient is in her eighties. Lives in an old, run-down house. Her health, especially her heart, gives cause for concern. She's on digoxin but I doubt if she always remembers to take her medication. And she's flatly refused meals on wheels.'

'How does she manage to get her shopping in? Or doesn't she?' Andrew's dark brow quirked.

'Some kind of iffy arrangement with a young woman next door, Roxanne,' Cate said. 'She seems kind enough and Madeleine's given her a key apparently. But it's all most unsatisfactory. I mean, Roxanne could walk in one day and find, well, anything.'

Peter came in practically. 'You could arrange with the aged-care assessment team from the PA hospital to pay her a visit, Cate. They'll recommend some kind of sheltered accommodation if it's warranted, and Mrs Twigg will just have to accept it.'

'I've thought of that.' Cate bit her lip. 'But it seems like putting pressure on an elderly person. She's such a proud old lady. Independent to a fault—'

'What're your options?' Andrew's deep voice cut in.

Cate flexed her fingers. 'Actually, there's a new nursing home at Chelmer I've heard of. I've spoken to the manager and there are still some vacancies. Madeleine would have her own room and everything's provided. She'd manage it on her pension with a bit left over. But getting her there?' Cate gave a shrug.

'At her age, she's possibly quite fearful of change,' Andrew said quietly. 'Would it help if we took her along to look at the place?'

Cate was taken aback by his direct approach, his willingness to become involved. The unsettling thought struck her that she knew almost nothing about Andrew Whittaker, the man.

'When do you intend to visit Mrs Twigg again?'

She coloured faintly, realising he was genuinely waiting for her answer. But did she want him looking over her shoulder like this? On the other hand, did she really have a choice? She swallowed. 'Perhaps Monday afternoon?'

'Suits me.' Tipping his head, he willed her to acknowledge him.

She did, feeling the ripple of awareness again, the tap-dance of her heart against her ribs. 'OK...' She got hurriedly to her feet. 'We'll arrange details later. Now, if everyone will excuse me?' She pushed her chair in. 'I've a hospital visit I must make.'

*   *   *

A vivid display of stocks, sweet peas and winter roses met Cate's gaze as she alighted from her car in the doctors' car park and made her way into the hospital through a rear entrance. She took a deep breath, glad to be in the anonymity of the large hospital away from— Damn. Why on earth did she feel so out of kilter? Muddled? Almost afraid?

Her patient was in the maternity section of St Anne's, an immense complex of both private and public facilities run by the Sisters of Mercy. As Cate took the lift to the third floor and made her way along to the nurses' station, the cloak of familiarity dropped over her.

It didn't seem all that long ago since she'd done her obstetrics rotation here. They'd been good times, she recalled, her mouth pinching into a wry smile.

'Cate, is that you?' Lyn Scali, the RN in charge, hailed her from behind a huge bank of mixed flowers and greenery. 'We've had our first set of triplets in two years born this morning.' She indicated the array of blooms. 'These just came for the new mum. Some women's magazine, I believe. Sole rights for the story and all that.'

Cate rolled her eyes. 'Celebrity status for the kids already, is it?' She leant on the counter. 'What's new, anyway, Lyn?'

'Babies?' Lyn gave a cryptic little smile. 'You here to see Kelly Davenport?'

'Just popping in on her,' Cate said.

'The consultant's quite pleased with her.' Lyn pulled the notes. 'But she'll need to rest at home.'

'Mmm.' Cate studied the file. 'I was concerned about the possibility of pre-eclampsia. She was retaining water like mad and miserable with headaches.'

'Looks like she's carrying a whopper,' Lyn mused.

'And she still has three weeks to go.'

The RN shook her head. 'She'll never make it. I'd take a bet we'll see her back by the middle of next week.'

'Then I'll bow to your undisputed in-
stincts,' Cate said with a grin. 'Thanks,
Lyn. I'd better push on.'

'I believe you have a new man at
Ferndale.' Lyn delayed her with an arch
smile.

Cate felt the heat crawl up the back of
her neck. 'How did you know?'

'I've been talking to Claire.'

'I'd forgotten you two were friends.'

'Well?' Lyn coaxed in exasperation.
'What's he like?'

'OK, I guess. Seems to know what he's
doing.'

'Please!' Lyn's laugh tinkled. 'I'll see for
myself, anyway. Claire's invited me to the
Maguires' farewell party.'

'Oh, right.' Involuntarily, Cate took in
Lyn's auburn good looks, feeling her heart
crank up a beat. The RN was probably
more Andrew Whittaker's type anyway.
Cate fluttered a wave. 'I'd better get on,
Lyn.'

'Sure. See you.' Lyn smiled, her look faintly puzzled as she watched her contemporary walk away.

Cate made her way to the four-bed ward, walking in and giving a friendly greeting to the women snugly settled under their bright counterpanes.

'How are you feeling, Kelly?' Cate pulled up a chair and sat beside her patient.

The young woman grimaced. 'Better than when I saw you yesterday. Thanks again for coming to the house. Dr Wyse said I can probably go home tomorrow morning,' she added brightly.

'To what?' Cate was blunt. 'More chasing after young Tim? Looking after an active two-year-old is not the best medicine for you at the moment, Kelly.'

'I know.' The young mother curled a strand of her bright red hair around her finger. 'I've talked to my sister-in-law. She's not working at the moment. She's happy to come over each day to keep an eye on both of us. And Anton's boss said he can start his holidays as soon as the baby's born.'

'Good thinking.' Cate smiled. 'You realise you could be a bit early, Kelly?'

'Mmm. Dr Wyse said I should be prepared and I'm all packed.' She chewed on her bottom lip. 'My waters broke at home with Tim. Should I expect the same this time?'

'Certainly expect it.' Cate got to her feet and placed her chair back against the wall. 'But no two pregnancies are exactly the same. Just make sure you've got some super-absorbent pads and a few towels handy to make your journey to the hospital more comfortable if your waters do break.'

Kelly giggled. 'Last time it was a bit of a nightmare. Anton and I were such babes in the woods. Neither of us knew quite what was happening. To make matters worse, I got the shakes and couldn't do a thing.'

'Joys of parenthood.' Cate touched a hand to the other's shoulder. 'Be ready anyhow. You may follow the same pattern with all your babies.'

'Oh, this is definitely the last one!' Kelly wrapped her arms across her stomach. 'Anton's agreed to a vasectomy.'

Cate held back a chuckle, knowing from experience that with the arrival of a healthy baby, and the joy and excitement that usually followed, couples had been known to change their minds about a rather permanent method of birth control.

Cate worked her way slowly through her afternoon surgery.

Her last appointment was with a new patient, fifty-year-old Beris Russell. Mrs Russell was seeking advice to help manage her menopause.

'I'm not about to take hormones, Doctor.' Beris Russell was direct. 'I've been told they cause weight gain.'

Cate lifted a hand and tucked a strand of hair behind her ear. Same old story, she thought. 'Mrs Russell,' she began, but the woman stopped her.

'Please, call me Beris.'

'Very well.' Cate smiled. 'But before we discuss hormone replacement therapy, why don't you tell me a bit about your lifestyle and how the menopause is affecting you?'

As she leant forward to listen to her patient, Cate noticed that Beris was well dressed, her hair and make-up tastefully done. That was a plus already. Although menopause was a natural phase in a woman's life, many had told Cate they'd felt awful and as a result hadn't been bothered with how they'd looked.

'I work at the Sandstrom Gallery in the city,' Beris Russell said. 'I'm a kind of assistant to the curator and I love my job.' She swallowed. 'I wouldn't like to lose it.'

Cate looked at her keenly. 'Is that a possibility?'

Beris lifted a shoulder. 'My confidence is shot to pieces with these hot flushes. Normally, I'm a vital kind of person, but lately I've been so forgetful.' She stopped and sent Cate a trapped smile. 'Would you believe I posted my wallet along with the gallery mail the other day?'

'Did you get it back?' Cate bit down on her bottom lip, stopping a grin.

'Fortunately.' Her look was wry. 'I fully intended seeing this through on my own, you know. But after that little incident, well, I decided to seek professional help.'

'Good.' Cate nodded. 'Because there is quite a lot we can do nowadays to relieve some of the uncomfortable stages of menopause. And don't be put off by random information about HRT, Beris. Granted, it's not for everyone but you shouldn't discount the positives either.'

'What about gaining weight, though?' Beris pressed. 'Is that true?'

Cate explained, 'Progestogen, one of the two female replacement hormones, can, in fact, slow normal bowel activity. But if you eat a balanced diet, perhaps forgo the big meal at night and eat something lighter, it can help. And exercise is very beneficial. It doesn't mean you have to tog up and go to the gym. Walking is wonderful.' Cate smiled. 'It's cheap, too.'

'I do like to walk. So, Doctor—' Beris looked thoughtful '—if I do what you're suggesting, could I try HRT?'

'You could try it, yes.' Cate was cautious. 'But first I'll need to take your medical history and give you a complete physical to ascertain whether you're a suitable candidate.'

The patient seemed happy enough with that. 'Could you do it today?'

With the merest glance at her watch, Cate saw her hopes for a reasonably early end to her working day fly out the window. But it would be remiss to send Beris away, especially as the woman had obviously steeled herself to keep the appointment in the first place.

'Certainly.' Cate smiled, beginning to explain what her patient could expect in the way of a physical.

'A mammogram as well?' Beris looked startled.

'When did you last have one?'

'Not for a while, actually,' she admitted.

'I'll give you a note for that.' Cate pulled her referral pad towards her. 'The Wesley is about the closest for you and they'll look after you very well. You'll just need to ring and make an appointment.' Cate brought her head up. Her patient had gone very still. 'Is that a problem?'

'No...' Beris shook her head. 'I was just thinking. It's all rather involved, isn't it?' She gave a small grimace. 'I thought per-haps we'd just have a chat and you'd give me a script or something...'

Cate went on writing. 'That wouldn't give you a satisfactory outcome, now, would it?'

'Of course not.' Beris was quick to agree. 'And don't get me wrong, Dr Clifford. I'm really grateful for all the care you're taking.'

Determined to get her paperwork up to date, Cate stayed on after her patient had gone, guessing that, apart from Pam Vickers, their cleaner, she was the only one left in the building.

It had been an odd kind of day, she reflected wryly, and she didn't have to look far for the reason. Suddenly she put her pen down and stretched, rotating her head to ease the muscles at the back of her neck.

Andrew Whittaker had upset the tenor of her day in no small measure. Perhaps she was still feeling vulnerable, a bit defensive around men.

Get over it, Cate, she scolded herself. It's months since you broke things off with

Rick. It's time you were back on track. She laughed self-derisively. Being free and almost thirty had nothing to do with it. Instinctively, she knew she still wasn't ready to get back in the swim.

Stretching her arms to half-mast, she glanced at her watch and blinked. Time to call it a day. Slowly she got to her feet and moved towards the window, looking out. The winter afternoon was drawing in, hovering between daylight and dusk, the rich colours of the sunset emblazoned across the canvas of pale sky.

Lost in thought, it took Cate a moment to register the movement in the car park beyond. It appeared to be a man running towards the surgery. One hand was clutched to his chest, wrapped in what looked like a blood-soaked towel.

'Dear God...' Cate breathed, flying to unlock the back door. 'What's happened?' she called sharply. She could see now that the man was young, with fair hair tied back in a ponytail.

'My hand...' He was out of breath, obviously shocked.

Cate stood back, ushering him inside. 'I'm Cate. I'm a doctor here. What's your name?'

He grimaced. 'Graeme Wood. Hell, it hurts...'

'Come through,' Cate said briskly. 'I'll take a look.' He seemed disorientated and she had almost to push him through the door of the treatment room. Getting him onto the couch, she directed a light on to the wound.

As she unwrapped the towel, Cate winced. The cut was deep and jagged. 'How did you do it, Graeme?'

He bit down hard on his bottom lip. 'I'm a chef at the restaurant down the road. I was deboning a chicken. Knife slipped.'

Cate disposed of the bloodied towel and used gauze to pack the wound temporarily.

'It's going to need cleaning and stitching, I'm afraid,' she told her patient. 'And you certainly can't go back to work tonight.'

He made a weak protest. 'Friday's our busiest night—'

'Well, they'll just have to manage without you.' Cate was firm. 'Are you a patient here?'

Graeme Wood shook his head. 'I saw cars parked outside. Thought someone might still be here.' In obvious pain he drew in a breath and clenched his teeth. 'Can you stitch me up, Doc?'

Cate nodded, her smile a bit rueful as she saw her working day extending even further. But what choice did she have? She could hardly bundle the poor man out to wait in one of the city's A and E departments for goodness knew how long.

'Back in a tick.' Cate pushed herself away from the treatment couch. 'I'll need to get some details from you first.'

It was totally quiet as Cate made her way along the corridor to Reception. Pam must have finished or be on a break, she decided, hurriedly pushing through the swing doors and gathering up the necessary forms to begin a new patient file.

Absorbed in her task, she didn't hear the soft footfall behind her.

'Cate?' the deep voice said. 'What are you doing here?'

CHAPTER THREE

CATE brought her head up, startled. 'Andrew...' She swallowed thickly. 'I thought everyone had gone.'

'Everyone but us, apparently. I've been in Pete's office, struggling through the idiosyncrasies of the computer system.'

And being darned quiet about it. Cate's mouth tightened. 'Did you manage?'

He grinned. 'Tell you this time next week. If I haven't chucked the whole lot out the window by then.' He propped himself on the counter beside her. 'Not still working, are you?'

'Emergency patient.' Cate grimaced. 'Young chef from a nearby restaurant. Knife wound.'

Andrew winced. 'Have you finished?'

'I wish!' She turned to leave. 'In fact, just about to start.'

He was right behind her as she brushed through the swing doors. 'Like another pair of hands?'

Cate tensed. Having him breathe down her neck while she worked was a prospect she didn't relish at all. 'Thanks, but I'll manage. Besides, you're not officially on duty yet.'

He raised the briefest smile. 'You could've fooled me.'

Cate felt the first stirrings of unease as his narrowed gaze appraised her. 'Perhaps, then, all the more reason for you to call it a day.'

They had come to a halt and were standing in the corridor, facing each other.

'I'd be happy to help out,' he persisted. 'I've had a light day. You, on the other hand, look whacked.'

Make that tired, dull, uninteresting, Cate interpreted. She tossed her head up. 'Don't presume to organise my workload, Andrew.'

'Is that what I'm doing?'

Cate's eyes clouded with confusion and she wondered why she was making such a mountain out of a molehill. But she knew all right, and she just wanted him gone, out of her orbit, so she could think straight.

Instead, she was trapped with him, scared of his proximity and of the power of the sensations coursing through her.

'Cate, let me help.'

She felt the catch in her breath when his touch on her arm turned to something else and he aligned himself in front of her, his hands cupping her face.

Shock widened her eyes. This shouldn't be happening, her head protested, but her heart wasn't listening.

'Andrew?' She said his name huskily, questioning, disbelieving.

'Don't fight this, Cate.' His voice had dropped to a hoarse compulsion. Before

Cate could move or protest, his mouth descended softly, exquisitely, against hers, the effect curling warmth and languor through her veins and right down to her toes.

A tremor ran all over her as he drew slowly back and looked at her. She licked her lips, felt the full weight of his blue eyes as they studied her. She swallowed. 'What…did that prove?'

He lifted a hand, letting his knuckles trail over her cheek. 'Perhaps only time will tell.' His eyes glittered momentarily before he half turned, plucking the file from her nerveless fingers. 'Now…' He gave her a triumphant little smile. 'Let's get this poor coot sorted, shall we, Doctor?'

'Arrogant toad,' Cate muttered, feeling thoroughly manipulated as she marched behind him to the treatment room.

'If you'll assist, I'll suture,' he said authoritatively.

Cate glared. 'Need the practice, do you?'

'Probably.' He lifted a shoulder casually.

Watching his broad back as he scrubbed, the ripple of taut muscle, Cate gave in to a reluctant smile and began to prepare a suture trolley.

Gowned and gloved, Andrew infiltrated the patient's wound with lignocaine and waited for it to go numb. 'Could no one from your work have come with you, Graeme?' he asked.

'Nah.' The young man shook his head. 'They'd have thought I was a wimp.'

Andrew met Cate's gaze in a speaking look. 'Of course, there was the odd chance you could have fainted from loss of blood,' he said drily.

'No worries, Doc. I knew someone would be able to help me.'

Almost an hour later, Andrew tied the last suture and straightened back to survey his work.

'You're good.' Cate was generous in her praise. In fact, he was more than good. Skilfully, and meticulously, he'd brought the edges of the cut together. Almost with a surgeon's precision, Cate decided, sealing the whole area with plastic skin to prevent infection.

Andrew stripped off his gloves. 'Come back in a week for a check-up,' he instructed his patient. 'It's possible the sutures will be able to come out by then. And try to keep them dry.'

Expertly, Cate tied a sling, elevating Graeme's hand against his chest. 'That should keep you more comfortable,' she said.

'I expect you'll be insured with Work Cover.' Andrew began releasing the tabs on his gown. 'But you'll need to take that up with your employer. I'll provide a certificate for the time you'll be off work. In fact...' he looked around him '...I'll do that now. Back shortly.'

'I...feel a bit shaky,' Graeme admitted, as Cate draped a blanket around his shoulders.

'Of course you do.' She looked keenly at him. 'You've had a shock. Now, is there someone at home to keep an eye on you?'

Graeme tried his weight tentatively. 'Girlfriend.' He sent Cate a crooked smile. 'She's a nurse.'

'Then you're in good hands.' She looked up as Andrew returned.

He handed Graeme his certificate and some painkillers. 'These are just to get you over the next few days,' he instructed. 'Any problems, contact the surgery—OK?'

'Thanks again, Doc.' Graeme took a couple of steps, swaying slightly. 'Do you reckon you could call a cab to get me home? I don't feel a hundred per cent.'

'I'll do that,' Cate offered, and hurried back to her office.

'Quite a day,' Andrew said later, as they turned to go inside, the cab containing their patient having just pulled away.

'And long.' Cate felt drained, both physically and mentally. Pushing open the door of the surgery, she came to an abrupt halt, blinking as the light hit her.

There was an awkward little silence when Andrew turned from locking the door. Cate linked her hands in front of her, waiting, watching him.

His throat muscles moved into a taut swallow. 'Will you allow me to buy you dinner, Cate?'

'Won't Peter and Ellie be expecting you?' Cate heard her voice strangely calm and wondered fleetingly how it was possible when her equilibrium had been turned on its head.

Andrew shoved his hands into his back pockets. 'I told Ellie I'd make my own arrangements. They've probably gone to the hospital, anyway, to see Bart.'

Cate considered this. 'Well, I guess eating out would be preferable to having cheese on toast at home.'

'Is that a yes?'

Instantly, Cate decided it would be both childish and churlish to refuse his invitation—and what harm could it do, anyway? She nodded. 'Thanks. I'd like to.'

'I, uh, don't know my way round yet,' he said gruffly. 'I'll leave it to you to choose a restaurant, bearing in mind I'm wearing jeans.'

'Damn.' Cate tapped her chin as though deep in thought. 'Bang goes somewhere posh.' She sent him a dry little smile. 'Leave it to me, Doctor. I know just the place. Now, give me two minutes to make myself presentable.'

'Only two?'

Cate heard the laugh in his voice as he called after her. Half turning, she showed him the tip of her tongue, the glow in her heart warmed even further by the sound of his spontaneous chuckle.

They met in the corridor outside Cate's consulting room. She'd done a quick make-up repair, swiped a brush through her hair and added a spray of her favourite cologne. She'd looked in the mirror and seen only wide-eyed vulnerability.

'All set?' Andrew's eyes rested approvingly on her and he smiled. 'It's ages since I've done this, Cate.'

She blinked. ''Gone out to dinner?'

'No...' And the word was almost lost in huskiness. 'Gone out with a woman.'

They left by the rear door, setting the alarm as they went. Cate carried her oatmeal jacket that matched her trousers. The night was so mild that a coat was hardly necessary, she thought, flicking a glance at Andrew. She noticed he'd replaced the Arran-type jumper he'd been wearing earlier in the day with a dark navy jacket.

'Had it in my car,' he said, interpreting her look.

'Beautiful night, isn't it?' Cate looked skywards to where the fat butter moon and necklace of stars looked close enough to touch.

'Mmm.' Andrew followed her gaze. 'Sure beats Canberra in winter.'

'Is that where you've been?'

'Off and on,' he dissembled, stopping beside his dark green Audi. 'I imagine you'll want to take your own car so I'll follow.'

Cate's arms tightened across the jacket she held in front of her. 'I rang and booked at a local restaurant, Galileo's. It's not far.'

'OK.' He touched the remote locking button on his keyring to open his door. 'See you there.'

As she drove, Cate tried to blank her mind and concentrate on the Friday night traffic. But it proved useless. Every few seconds she found herself going back, refocusing on Andrew Whittaker and the way he'd erupted into her life.

There was parking available in a side street near the restaurant and they managed to find places within several metres of each other.

Galileo's had been reconstructed from an old grocery store, with a new section spilling out to an atrium. It was there that Andrew and Cate were shown to a table for two and quite close to where a large pot-bellied stove provided a gentle warmth to the patrons.

'This all looks very civilised,' Andrew said in approval.

'Brisbane has quite an upmarket café scene now.' Cate took the chair he held for her. 'Galileo's is one of my favourites.'

Within seconds a waiter was hovering.

'We're both driving.' Cate's brow puckered over the drinks list.

Andrew sent her a measured smile. 'I guess a glass of the house red wouldn't put us over the legal limit, would it? And something to start,' he added. 'I don't know about you but I'm starving.'

'Some herb bread might be nice,' she agreed.

Their orders given, they sat back and surveyed each other.

'Well, Cate Clifford...' He smiled, breaking the sharp twist of tension between them. 'Here we are.'

'Yes.' Blinking a bit uncertainly, Cate looked around her. There was a sheen on the leaves of the tall indoor plants dotting the perimeter of the atrium, the fairy lights strung between them twinkling like tiny stars.

Strangely unnerved, she looked down at her hands clasped across her lap. The warm intimacy of the restaurant was suddenly disturbing in its potency, in some way bringing her close to him, making her aware of him in a way she could hardly comprehend.

With only the width of the table between them, she could have reached out and touched him. It shook her even more to realise she desperately wanted to.

'You've gone very quiet.' Andrew's gaze travelled over her face and dropped to the curve of her breast.

'Just unwinding.' Cate bit her tongue on the lie, her hand stealing up to her throat as if to protect herself from his unwavering scrutiny. 'Do you think you're going to like working in general practice?' It was ridiculous and mundane but it was the best she could do.

'What's not to like?' He shrugged. 'I've done my GP training so it's only a matter of getting back to it. But to answer your question, yes. I'm looking forward to covering for Pete. Have you been at Ferndale long?'

'Six months.' She looked up and thanked the waiter as he placed their wine on the table.

'Your first stint as a GP?'

'Heavens, no! I was in a group practice at St Lucia before that.'

'St Lucia?' Andrew looked at her over the rim of his glass. 'Isn't that the location of the Queensland University?'

She nodded, feeling suddenly trapped as memories of her association with Rick De Lisle came flooding back.

'It didn't suit you?'

Andrew's voice seemed to come from a long way off. Cate quickly gathered herself. 'It was a large practice. Too many egos to massage.' Her fingers trembled slightly as she placed them on the stem of her glass. 'I'm much happier at Ferndale. Cheers.' She raised her glass, her small chin tilting as if in cool dismissal of further probing.

Some history there, Andrew decided, his gaze thoughtful. Cate Clifford had acted almost panicky. Like a small creature confused by headlights. Perhaps one day she'd trust him enough to tell him about it.

Their herb bread arrived and Andrew set about it as though he hadn't eaten in a week.

Having recovered her poise, Cate looked on amusedly. 'What did you have for lunch?' she asked, nibbling on a crisp edge.

'Some kind of fish thing.' His grin was a bit lopsided. 'Am I being a pig?'

She shook her head. Just the opposite, and it was rather endearing to watch a grown man exact such enjoyment from a simple meal.

'Ever been married, Cate?'

Her gaze became shuttered. 'No. You?'

'No.' He wiped his fingers on his serviette. 'I never seemed to be in one place long enough to devote time to anyone special.'

Recklessly, Cate wondered why that pleased her. 'I imagine it must be rather a scary experience when you're deployed to a disaster zone.'

'Of course,' he said briefly. 'But very often you get very little notice and you're there in the thick of it before you know it.'

'Why did you want to join the army?' Cate was frankly puzzled.

'Perhaps a notion I had to help those less fortunate. Test myself, utilise my skills. But the lifestyle isn't for everyone and I'd be foolish to think it doesn't take its toll. I was just back from a peace-monitoring stint in Bougainville when I was deployed to the tidal wave in New Guinea.' He shook his head. 'That wasn't a good time.'

Cate looked at him through the fringe of her lashes. It was obvious his experiences had deeply affected him. Were still affecting him. 'How long since you left the army?'

'Couple of weeks.' Without warning his hand reached out and covered hers. 'It wasn't all tough going. When I wasn't attached to a specific task force, I did routine stuff. Had a chance to see lots of interesting places along the way.'

'But you were glad to leave?'

'Yes... I think so...'. Slowly, he began to separate her fingers with his thumb, touching the tip of each one as he moved across her hand. 'Everyone has their limits. Don't you agree?'

She nodded, unable to speak. Every nerve in her body tightened, became electrified with sensation. She stared down at the hand covering hers. His skin was a natural smooth olive, his fingers long, blunt-tipped. And she had an overwhelming desire to be touched all over by them. Stroked. Loved—

'Would you like to order now?' The waitress materialised, pad at the ready, and smiled.

Andrew seemed to gather himself, removing his hand slowly from Cate's. 'Let's.' He picked up the menu, massaging a finger across his forehead as if making a conscious effort to concentrate. 'Everything looks good,' he said. 'And I'm famished.'

'Still?' Cate took refuge in humour. 'You've just demolished almost an entire loaf of bread. You must have hollow legs.'

'Don't think so.' He looked up and gave her a very sweet smile. 'I'd have noticed.'

CHAPTER FOUR

SATURDAY morning.

Cate woke with a feeling of well-being, something she hadn't experienced for weeks. Was it all because of Andrew Whittaker? Just for a moment her heart thumped wildly in her chest.

Blinking, she looked up at the ceiling, her mind drifting back to last night when she and Andrew had left the restaurant.

The temperature had dropped and he'd helped her on with her jacket, then clasped her hand in his as they'd walked to their cars.

She'd bent to unlock the door on her Polo and then had turned to him. 'Good-night, Andrew. Thanks for a lovely evening.'

'Thank *you*, Cate,' he'd said, turning her towards him. They'd come together almost in slow motion.

She hadn't been able to see his face clearly but she'd caught his male scent as he'd bent to her. He'd kissed her once, twice, three times, a series of fleeting, tantalising enquiries. 'Sleep well,' he'd said, handing her into her car...

'For heaven's sake!' Cate muttered, throwing back the duvet. So Andrew Whittaker had kissed her. So what?

He'd already said he'd not been out with a woman in ages, she rationalised, pulling on her dark blue dressing-gown. He was obviously intent on trying to make every post a winner. It didn't mean anything special. Besides, Cate thought, ruffling her hair as she padded through to the kitchen, she wasn't looking for any deep involvement either.

It was a fabulous morning, Cate realised, sitting over her breakfast. She'd sliced some succulent rock melon, made tea and toast and taken it all out on a tray to her sundeck.

It was heaven to have the weekend off. Cate spread her toast with marmalade and then sat back to enjoy it. Her gaze went upwards to where the sky was a canopy of blue, the clear, soft blue of winter in south-east Queensland.

She had so much to be grateful for. Warming her hands around her tea-mug, she lifted it to her mouth, hearing the soft cooing of several wood doves in the shrubbery beside the railings. Cate smiled gently. They were probably nest-building—or at least thinking about it—now that spring was so close.

Her mouth drew in and she placed her mug back on the table. She went suddenly still. She and Rick had planned a springtime wedding.

Well, it was never going to happen now. Standing quickly, she gathered up her tray, realising she should be glad she'd found him out in time. And she was. But now and then it all came back, leaving her feeling hurt all over again. Foolish. Poor, trusting Cate.

Determinedly, she sloughed off her introspection, placing her used crockery in the dishwasher. It was time to grab a quick shower and head off to Bea's school fête.

She hadn't done this in ages, Cate thought. Attended a school fête, that was. A ripple of lightness ran through her as she dressed in white cargo pants and a white cotton jumper. Her skin was looking quite good these days, she decided, smoothing on a light foundation and outlining her mouth with a soft pink lipstick.

Bending her head, she swept her tangle of blond hair up into a ponytail. Her last bit of preparation was to knot an apricot-coloured lightweight jumper around her shoulders.

Two minutes later, she slammed her front door and set out to walk the two blocks to the venue.

Cate found herself being swept up in the general excitement as she entered the primary school grounds. The stalls were set out in a semicircle around the quadrangle, gaily striped bunting and balloons enticing the patrons to explore further and hopefully spend their money.

She looked around her, absorbing the atmosphere, listening to the children's happy shrieks and laughter. Well, they certainly had enough to keep them occupied. Cate smiled, returning the wave of an outgoing little four-year-old as he glided past on the merry-go-round.

Her stomach dipped. She wanted children. But that prospect was on hold now. Thanks to Rick… She sighed softly. Surely it was time to let the anger go? She bit her lip, moving on past the rides and the red and yellow jumping castle where the youngsters were having a grand time trampolining and sliding over the cushioned shapes.

'Cate!' She looked up to see Bea beckoning her. Fluttering a wave, Cate made her way across to the cake stall.

She was promptly put to work. 'If you could give me an hour or so?' Bea asked hopefully. 'Just until my next helper can get here.'

Cate chuckled. 'Glad to, Bea.' Slipping off her canvas shoulder-bag, she surveyed the array of cakes, slices and biscuits. 'Someone's been busy.'

'People have been wonderful.' Bea placed a luscious-looking strawberry and cream sponge to the front of the counter. 'Now, everything's marked,' she rushed on. 'Change in the tin here. I'll have to leave you for a tick. I've got to collect a box of goodies someone's left in one of the classrooms.'

Business was brisk and Cate couldn't believe how quickly the time passed. By eleven o'clock, Bea's other helper had arrived and Cate prepared to vacate the stall.

'What are you going to do now?' Bea placed a friendly hand on her arm.

Cate hesitated. 'Probably take a wander through the rest of the stalls,' she said. 'I'd rather like to buy some home-made jam.'

'Over there.' Bea indicated the candy-striped awning across the way. 'There's bound to be loads.'

Cate's hand was on the jar of strawberry jam when a shadow fell across her. She looked up, startled, and swallowed as she saw Andrew's face.

'Hello, Cate,' he said, his hands on his lean hips as he looked quizzically down at her.

'Andrew…' Cate blinked, her cheeks flushing. 'What are you doing here?'

His blue eyes glinted and he grinned. 'Ellie had made some cakes for Bea's stall.

I offered to drop them off. She and Pete had some last-minute business at the travel agent's. What's that you're looking at?'

Cate grimaced. 'Home-made jam. I'm trying to decide between strawberry, apple and strawberry or ginger marmalade.'

'Good grief.' Andrew shook his head slightly. 'It's terrifying, the decisions we have to make in our lives, isn't it?' He sent Cate a dry smile. 'Let's make it easy and buy the lot.' He began reaching for his wallet. 'It's all in a good cause.'

Cate felt decidedly outmanoeuvred as he paid for the jam and held the brown paper bag towards her. 'Now I'll have to come round and help you eat it.'

'Will you, now?' Cate felt herself laughing softly at the hopeful sound in his voice.

His laugh was self-deprecating. 'Didn't fool you for a minute, did I, Doctor?'

As if in silent mutual consent, they strolled off together, stopping occasionally to admire the various displays, the urban mix of talents. Someone had donated a beautiful lace tablecloth to be raffled, and next door some year sevens tried hopefully to interest the crowd in their pottery and painting efforts.

'Bring back memories?' Somehow, Andrew's arm found its way around her shoulders and slowly, gently, he eased her towards him.

Cate nodded. This is crazy, she thought, but somehow she couldn't tear herself away, functioning automatically as they continued their tour. They bought icy poles and slurped them like greedy children, and Andrew won a sack of potatoes which he promptly donated back.

Cate tutted. 'You could've had chips for six months.'

'And high cholesterol for twelve,' he snorted. 'Ah, look!' He tugged her towards yet another stall. 'Knock 'ems. Like a go?'

Cate eyed the small wooden balls doubtfully. 'Think I'll leave it to you.'

'Chicken.' He sent her a lazy grin. 'OK, let's take it and shake it, as they say.'

Cate sniffed disdainfully, trying not to notice the easy flex of his shoulders, the whipcord strength in his arms as he threw. And won.

'What would you like?' The stall operator smiled broadly at them.

'Lady's choice.' Andrew spread his hands magnanimously.

Cate bit her lip, vaguely embarrassed. 'What, uh, is there?'

'Everything you could wish for.' Laughing, the stall operator waved a hand at the shelves. 'Let's see. There are chocolates, tins of biscuits, cans of lager—'

'Ah!' Andrew raised dark brows hopefully.

'Not on your life.' Cate gave a cracked laugh. 'I'll have one of the knitted toys,' she decided. 'The little owl.'

'Now, why would you have chosen that?' Andrew's eyes locked with hers, their colour becoming more bright as they reflected colour from his blue shirt.

Cate stroked her fingers over the brown-and-white-flecked soft toy, jauntily clad in a red waistcoat. 'It looked like it needed a home,' she said simply.

'I know the feeling.' He gave a hard, scoffing laugh before his jaw clamped, his expression unreadable.

Unnerved, Cate took a step back. The light atmosphere between them had vanished, as though a door had closed or a shadow had fallen suddenly and swiftly between them. For a few seconds Andrew Whittaker had looked...vulnerable. But why?

Did he need to talk about something? Cate immediately drew back from asking him. It would be presumptuous. They hardly knew each other.

'Come on,' she said instead, tucking the little owl under her arm. 'I'm buying lunch.'

The hamburgers were delicious, best beef smothered with onions. 'Heaven,' Cate sighed in satisfaction, consuming the last morsel.

'I could go another.' Andrew leant across, blotting the trace of sauce from her chin with a paper napkin. 'What about you?'

'No, thanks.' She coloured faintly. 'But you go ahead. Picking up her glass of wine and sipping the cool, dry liquid, she watched him as he waited his turn at the barbecue. A man of many parts—was that what he was?

Then he was back, tucking his long legs under the picnic table they were sharing. 'How's the wine?' He sent her a look from under his brows.

'Lovely.' Cate ran the pad of her thumb across the stem of her glass. 'You should have had some.'

'I'm driving,' he said. 'Alcohol in the middle of the day lays me right out in any case.'

'Even one glass of wine?' Cate was sceptical.

'You'd better believe it.' He gave her a very candid look. 'Are you busy this afternoon?'

'Why?' Cate met his eyes for the longest time, watching as their tawny flecks splintered their blue setting, making them a mixture of amber and green. A tiger's eyes, she thought. Ever watchful. She licked her lips. 'What did you have in mind?'

'I've a couple of flats to look at. Wondered if you might lend me your local knowledge.'

'I thought you'd be staying on at the Maguires',' she said, evading the suggestion.

He shook his head. 'I don't need all that space. By anyone's standards it's a huge house. Even Pete and Ellie realise it's too big for them now the girls have left home.' He downed the last few mouthfuls of his soft drink. 'I just need somewhere I can park myself for the next little while. I don't have much gear.'

Cate fell silent. It sounded such a loner's existence, so transient. 'Don't you want to put down some roots?'

He gave a grunt of laughter. 'You sound like Ellie.'

'Well, it's a fairly normal assumption.' Cate bristled slightly. 'When you get to a certain age, I mean.'

He stared at her, his fingers flexing, aching to free her hair from its ponytail. The thought of its silkiness gliding through his fingers was enough to set his body on fire.

He wanted her. It didn't shock him. But it probably would've shocked her. A hollow, self-derisive laugh jammed in his throat. If her pointed remarks about putting down roots was any indication of her thinking, he couldn't quite see Cate Clifford being accepting of a casual fling.

Desire drained away. 'Age has nothing to do with it, Cate.'

She shrank back into her space. He'd distanced her with a look, clamping his jaw. Almost, as if he was locking himself in, putting up the shutters. Cate swallowed. 'Are you OK, Andrew?'

He was conscious of her eyes on him, her voice persuasive in its concern. 'Yes, I'm fine. Just a bit preoccupied.'

Cate bit down on her bottom lip. It felt like another dismissal but she soldiered on. 'Tell me about these flats.' She made an attempt at lightness, hoping to get back onto his wavelength.

He made himself smile. 'Don't think I'll bother after all. There's plenty of time.' He sent his empty can flying into a nearby receptacle and got to his feet. 'Can I drop you anywhere?'

She looked up, her heartbeat suddenly fast, an agitated little flutter against the soft cotton of her jumper. 'Thanks. But I'm not quite ready to leave yet.'

'OK.' He dipped his head in a curt nod. 'I'll see you.'

Cate's thoughts were spinning as she watched him walk away, his broad shoulders straight, giving the impression of shutting her out, his hand coming up to thrust impatiently through his dark hair.

Well, he'd made a mess of that. A strained little smile quirked Andrew's mouth. Now she was probably wondering what kind of mixed-up idiot he was. But it had been wise to leave when he had. Things had been shaping up to become decidedly heavy.

Halfway to the exit he paused, watching the children from the infants' class performing their folk dancing, their little faces intent, their movements slightly uncoordinated.

Such innocence. Andrew shook his head and began to walk away. He felt about a hundred years old.

An announcement over the public address system had him jerking to a stop, pivoting and racing back to the amusement area.

An accident.

Two boys, eleven-year-old pupils of the school, had collided while trampolining and had taken a nasty tumble in the process.

Kids are resilient. Andrew kept the thought uppermost in his mind as he made his way through the gathering crowd to the scene.

Cate was there before him.

'What've we got?' Andrew asked tersely, hunkering down beside the injured lads. 'What?' He turned his head at Cate's little cry of alarm.

She bit her lip. 'This boy is Will Harrison.'

'Bea's son?' The boy was unconscious, his young body at a peculiar angle. 'Could someone get Mrs Harrison, please?' Andrew snapped the question. 'She'll be at the cake stall. And ice,' he yelled after the departing messenger.

'Oh, man— Brent!' A gangling red-haired youth dropped to his knees beside them, his face white with shock. 'Dad'll kill me. I was supposed to keep an eye on him...'

'Is Brent your brother?' Cate asked. Her first impressions of the boys' injuries were that they would require a trip to the hospital and for that parents or guardians would need to be located.

'Stepbrother.' The youth blinked rapidly. 'His arm looks all funny.'

'That's because his shoulder is dislocated,' Cate said quietly.

'Little idiot!' The youth's voice was a strangled sob. 'That's his bowing arm.'

Cate's sharp questioning look brought forth an emotive answer. 'He plays the violin.'

'Good grief...' Andrew muttered, and shook his head. 'Let's get some objectivity here, shall we? And a bit of triage, if that's possible. What have you got on Brent, Dr Clifford?'

Cate moved to comfort the whimpering youngster. 'As well as the shoulder, I'd say a suspected fracture of his cheekbone. His ankle's beginning to swell but is obviously not broken. Sprain more likely.'

'I feel sick...' As Cate held him, Brent turned his head and began to retch miserably.

'Oh, my God.' Bea Harrison burst through the bystanders, her face crumpling at the sight of her son's prostrate form. 'Cate? Andrew? Tell me!' Her stricken gaze shot from one doctor to the other. 'He's not...?' She came to a shuddering halt.

'Take it easy, Bea.' Andrew's even tone camouflaged his deep concern. The boy should have come round by now. 'It seems as though it's been one of those freak accidents that kids get involved in from time to time.'

'What are you telling me, Andrew?' With a huge effort Bea fought for—and found—control.

'It seems the lads collided in mid-air. Will was obviously out of it before he hit the ground.'

'Oh, Lord.' Bea shuddered. 'Look at his poor little back.' She'd lifted her son's T-shirt, frowning at the already darkening bruise.

'He must have hit the metal edge of the trampoline as he fell,' Cate said quietly. 'Bea, I'm so sorry.'

'The ambulance is on its way,' someone said.

'About time.' Andrew looked grim as he monitored his young patient's vital signs, noting that the boy's pulse was elevated but still strong. Please, heaven, it would result in nothing worse than concussion.

'Mum...'

'Oh, sweetheart, you're awake.'

'Gently, Bea,' Andrew cautioned, when the mother would have swept the injured child into her arms. 'Let's keep Will quiet just now, shall we?'

'Dr Clifford?'

Cate looked up to see Lauren Bentley hovering with a large bag of chipped ice. Cate felt blank for a moment until she remembered that this was the school Lauren was returning to teach at.

'I took it from the drinks cooler.' The young woman dropped to her knees beside Cate. 'And a couple of teatowels as well. I guessed you'd need something to wrap it in to make an ice pack.'

'That's wonderful, Lauren. Thank you.' Cate felt some of her tension drain away with the arrival of the extra pair of hands. And obviously competent ones at that. 'We'll need ice on Brent's cheekbone and ankle.'

'Young monkeys.' Swiftly, Lauren made ice mounds in the teatowels, grabbing the four corners and hoisting them up like Christmas puddings. She handed one to Cate. 'I'll take care of the ankle, shall I?'

Cate nodded gratefully, placing the ice pack gently on Brent's rapidly swelling cheek.

Lauren was equally gentle with his ankle. 'There you go, hotshot.' She sent the boy a wicked smile. 'I suppose this was some half-hearted attempt to slide off school on Monday, was it? You must have known I was coming back to teach you next week, hmm?'

Her pupil gave a weak smile. 'Is Dad coming?' he asked.

Lauren looked a question at Cate who answered guardedly, 'We've yet to sort that out, actually. His older brother's here somewhere, though.'

'That'll be Jared.' Lauren nodded. 'Nice lad. I know the family so I'll help co-ordinate if you like, Dr Clifford.'

'I'm sure we'd all be most grateful for your expertise, Lauren. And it's Cate—please.'

'How's Will?' The teacher's voice was hushed.

Cate swallowed. She'd sensed Andrew's concern, almost felt it through the pores of her skin. 'We'll know more when we get him to hospital.'

A hush fell over the gathering when the ambulance arrived, reversing slowly into the grounds to the scene of the accident.

'Right, let's get these kids on their way.' Relief showed on Andrew's face. He directed a sharp query at Cate. 'Where are we sending them, Doctor?'

'St Anne's.' Cate's reply was swift and unequivocal. 'They have an outstanding children's department. The boys will be in good hands.'

'If you'll go with Bea in the ambulance, I'll follow in my car,' he said. 'Any joy in locating Brent's parents?'

'His teacher is following it up. Meanwhile, perhaps Jared could go with you. Brent will need someone...'

'Absolutely.' Andrew's reply was quietly spoken. He was conscious of keeping a tight hold on his emotions. He hadn't needed this today. His mouth tightened. Children in pain brought back memories he'd rather have kept at bay...

'Afternoon, folks.' The ambulance officers alighted.

'We'll need a collar for this one, please.'

'Right you are, Doc. Got one about his size, I think.'

Under Andrew's careful supervision, the collar was fitted around Will Harrison's neck and he was gently and expertly transferred to a stretcher.

'OK, sport?' Andrew placed a hand on the youngster's fair head.

'I'm coming with you, darling.' Bea held tightly to her son's hand.

'Mum...' Will's voice was a frightened little whisper. 'I can't feel my legs...'

CHAPTER FIVE

'I'M SORRY your Saturday's been ruined, Cate,' Bea said for the umpteenth time. 'And Andrew's, too.'

'Bea, please.' Cate gave the older woman's hand a comforting squeeze. 'There's no way we were going to leave you here at the hospital on your own.' Cate's eyes went to her watch and she wondered just how much longer Andrew was likely to be. He'd insisted on accompanying the boys to the X-ray department, telling Bea he'd be back when he had some news on Will.

She could only hope and pray the news would be good.

'It would happen on the weekend Jeff is out of state,' Bea said with a little catch in her voice.

'You'll be able to contact him, though?'

'Yes. But I thought…' Her face worked for a minute. 'I thought I should wait until we know what's going on with Will.' She expelled a long sigh, staring ahead of her. 'Tell me truthfully, Cate. Is there a chance he'll be…paraplegic?'

Cate hid her unease. The truth was, she had no way of knowing. No doctor was God. They were mere mortals who could only make judgements on the facts and conditions presented at the time.

'Bea, I know it's hard, waiting,' she said. 'They'll be doing full X-rays on Will plus a CT scan of his head. It all takes time. But, please, don't start dwelling on the worst-case scenario. Look, why don't I get us a cup of coffee?'

Bea nodded. 'OK…'

When Cate got back with the hot drinks, Bea wasn't where she'd left her. Slightly alarmed, Cate sent her gaze around the waiting area, expelling a little breath of relief when she saw the mother over by the window, staring out.

Hurriedly, Cate put the coffee down and went to her. 'Bea?' She put a hand on the woman's shoulder and she turned. Immediately, Cate could see she'd been crying. Disquiet ripped through Cate. 'What is it? Has there been some news?'

'No.' Bea shook her head, palming the growing wetness away from her eyes. 'I...' She swallowed. 'I was just feeling sorry for myself. Picturing how it would be if Will can't—'

'Come on, now.' Cate used her most rallying tone. 'That's crazy talk. Will's a healthy child. The lack of feeling in his legs could be down to a number of possibilities. Here.' Cate pulled a wad of tissues from her shoulder-bag. 'Blow your nose and wipe your eyes. Will won't want to see his mum looking like a wet week, now, will he?'

Bea hiccuped a laugh, taking a shuddering breath. 'Thanks, Cate. You've been so kind.'

Cate clicked her tongue. 'Stop with the gratitude. Our Ferndale family sticks together. You told me that yourself, remember?'

Back in the waiting area, Bea sipped her coffee, making an obvious effort to compose herself. 'I'm glad Lauren managed to track down Brent's dad. Apparently, he was on the golf course.' She sighed. 'I only said two words to him. Perhaps I should—'

'Bea!' Cate sent the practice manager a stern look. 'Mr Walker is being well looked after by the staff. And I talked to him about Brent.'

Bea gnawed at her lip. 'I expect he was upset.'

'He did seem rather tense.' Cate recalled Neil Walker's almost brusque questions, his hands kneading his golf cap as he'd spoken to her. 'Brent and Jared are stepbrothers, I understand.'

'Brent's from his second marriage,' Bea confirmed. 'But the boys spend time together. Mostly at the weekends.'

Cate frowned. 'What about Brent's mother?'

'She died.' Bea looked down into her coffee. 'Breast cancer. About eighteen months ago.'

Cate drew in a thin breath. 'That's sad. How does Mr Walker manage?'

'Housekeeper during the week. Weekends they soldier on as best they can, I guess.'

There was silence then, both women occupied with their own thoughts. Finally Bea stirred. 'Will Andrew know where to find us? Sorry.' She made a small face. 'It's just that the waiting seems endless.'

'I know.' Cate was sympathetic. 'I'm sure he'll get here just as soon as he has something to tell us.'

And that looked as though it could be sooner rather than later. She stiffened as Andrew's distinctive dark head appeared briefly in the crowd spilling from a nearby lift.

'Bea.' Cate touched the other woman's arm. 'Andrew's just arrived.' She waved and waited for him to join them.

Andrew acknowledged the two women with a nod, pulling out a chair so that they sat in a semicircle.

'What's the prognosis?' Bea burst out, her voice reedy with apprehension.

'Relax, Bea.' Andrew leant across to cover both her hands with his. 'Your son is going to be OK.'

'Oh, thank God...' Bea's face crumpled.

'The paediatrician is of the opinion that the jolt to his back when he struck the edge of the trampoline was the cause of the temporary paralysis. Will suffered some slight nerve compression. It's just taking time to come good again,' Andrew said. 'But he's already getting feeling back.'

'Will they keep him in?' Bea wiped a hand across her eyes.

'At least overnight. Perhaps an extra day to make sure. They're settling him into the ward now.' Andrew smiled, his eyes crinkling at the corners. 'I'll take you up. The paediatrician would like a word with you as well.'

'Yes.' Bea pushed her hair back from her face, twirling a strand as if it helped her think. 'I'd better try to phone my husband.'

'Use my mobile.' Andrew took his phone from his back pocket and pushed it into the mother's hand.

'Do you have an update on Brent?' Cate asked, conscious of the awkward little silence that had fallen between them once Bea had stepped outside to use the phone.

'He's going to be fine.' Andrew lifted a hand and rubbed the back of his neck. 'Pretty sore, understandably, and a bit sorry for himself. His dad and Jared are with him now. Bea OK?' He changed tack, a question in his eyes. 'All this must have been very hard on her.'

'Especially with Jeff away,' Cate confirmed. 'It was nice of you to follow through for her.'

'The least I could do,' he said dismissively. 'From what I observed, you weren't exactly uninvolved yourself, Cate.'

His blue gaze scorched across her face and she made an impatient movement with her hand. 'I would've thought it came with the territory.'

Bea returned, looking as though the cares of the world had been lifted from her shoulders. 'Jeff's catching the next flight out of Sydney,' she said. 'He'll be home this evening. And he said to thank you both,' she added, a little catch in her voice. 'As I do...'

Cate took a cab home a little later. Andrew had offered her a lift if she'd cared to wait. She hadn't.

*   *   *

The telephone rang at nine-thirty that evening when Cate was thinking of tuning in to a late movie on cable television.

'It's me,' said Andrew, when she put the receiver to her ear.

Cate's heart picked up its rhythm. 'Is anything wrong?'

'No.' His husky expulsion of breath seemed nerve-tinglingly close. 'I wondered if I might come over?'

Cate's fingers tightened on the receiver. How had he got her number? Easily enough, she thought. Either from Peter or Ellie. Or Bea. And he'd have it anyway when he commenced officially at the surgery on Monday.

Why was she dithering like this? She could just say no. Agitatedly, she locked a hand in her hair now freed from its ponytail.

'Cate?'

'Ah, yes, OK, then,' she heard herself saying. 'Do you have my address?'

'Yes, I do.'

Cate's pulse began to race. He'd be here in a matter of minutes. The Maguires' home was only a few kilometres away.

Cate looked down at her fluffy slippers. Lord, she couldn't greet him like this! Earlier, she'd had a shower, washed her hair and changed into pyjamas and dressing-gown.

Her heart pounding, she tore upstairs, dispensed with her night attire and pulled on jeans and a pale blue jumper. There was no time to fiddle with make-up. Besides, she was off duty and at home. He could take her as he found her.

I don't believe I'm doing this, she thought, stifling a self-derisive laugh as she returned to the living area, plumping up cushions and putting on a CD of classical guitar music.

The mellow chime of her doorbell had her spinning around, hand on heart. She wanted to see him so badly it hurt. Oh,

Lord, this was ridiculous. Shaking her head as if to clear it, she went to let him in.

'Hello again,' he said. His smile was brief, his eyes strangely intense.

'Hello…' She saw he was wearing comfortable chinos and a dark-coloured sweater, the sleeves pushed up over his forearms. She stood back to allow him to come in, fearing her knees were about to buckle at the avalanche of sensation that flooded her.

'Got some cold milk to go with this?'

He'd obviously stopped at the bottle shop at the pub. Cate took the plastic bag he handed her. 'Oh, lovely!' Smiling broadly, she took out the bottle of imported liqueur. 'Kahlua, my favourite. Come through.' She waved a hand in the direction of the space allocated to the kitchen.

The living area of the apartment flowed into an open-plan design. 'Nice place.' Andrew strolled across the polished floorboards and parked himself on one of the high kitchen chairs at the serving bench. 'Been here long?'

'Years.' With neat, co-ordinated movements Cate assembled glasses, milk and ice cubes. 'Mum bought it for me when I began university.' She smiled wryly. 'It's had an update since then, of course.'

'And very effectively.' He looked approvingly around the white and vivid blue decor, the splash of yellow daisies making a homely contrast against the clinical stainless-steel fittings. 'And upstairs is what? Bedrooms, bathroom?'

'All of the above.' Intent on her task, Cate poured a measure of the liqueur over the ice cubes and topped the glasses with milk. 'Is this the kind of place you're looking for, Andrew?'

'God no,' he muttered gruffly, his arms folded, looking at her.

Cate's mouth tightened momentarily and she handed him his drink. Because it would be too much like putting down roots. Well, it was his choice where he lived. 'Shall we go through to the lounge?' she said, picking up her own drink and leading the way.

Cate lowered herself onto one of the two sofas, thinking he would take the other one. Instead, drink in hand, he began prowling around the room, stopping here and there to examine a picture, a book, even the mosaic tiles that surrounded her fireplace. Almost, she thought, as though he was seeking out the substance, the essential quality that was *home*.

The idea of that concerned her more than she was willing to admit. Even to herself.

'Is this your mother?' Turning to her, Andrew held a photograph in a plain pewter frame.

Cate swallowed, her eyes going to the image of the two women, their fair hair blowing in the wind. 'Yes,' she said. 'It was taken last Christmas. We were at the marina, waiting for my stepfather to moor our little runabout.'

'You're very alike.' Andrew placed the framed picture back where he'd found it. 'Do you have siblings?'

'I'm an only child. My father was killed when I was four. For a long time it was just Mum and I, and then when I began my internship she married my stepfather, Rod Kennard. It's turned out well for all of us. What about you?' Cate made her voice light, taking a mouthful of her drink and placing her glass on a side table.

'One sister, Helene. She's a journalist, working in Canberra.' Pulling a book from the shelf, he studied the flyleaf and placed it back. 'My parents have a property outside Canberra. I went to boarding school when I was fourteen and I did my medical training at St Vincent's in Sydney. Am I intruding on your space, Cate?'

She looked at him sharply and saw what seemed like lines of strain etched deeply in his face. Her world seemed to tilt and emotions she'd thought buried stirred within her. She wanted to go to Andrew Whittaker. Hold him. And a whole lot more.

Her thoughts spun wildly and she took a shaken breath. 'Andrew, are you all right?'

'You asked that this afternoon.' His quick smile lifted the harsh lines of concentration. 'I'm not at the end of my tether or anything like that, Cate. Tonight I just needed someone to talk to—not about anything specific.' He stopped abruptly.

'I'm glad you came, then.'

'Me, too.' The tension eased out of him and he finished off his drink.

Boldly, perhaps foolishly, Cate patted the seat beside her.

Andrew's dark brow lifted fractionally before he acted, dropping to the sofa beside her, tipping his head back. 'Talk to me, Cate.'

'I thought I had been.'

His gaze shifted to her hair spilling around her shoulders, gleaming in the soft light. 'Why is a nice girl like you not out and about on a Saturday night?' he asked.

She gave a rueful laugh. 'Saturday nights faded into oblivion about a week after I began as an intern.'

'I can empathise with that.' He held out his hand and for a moment her heart thumped wildly. He sent her a very blue look. 'This feels good, doesn't it?'

Cate nodded, conscious of the way her hand nestled in his as though it belonged.

'Thank you, Cate.'

'For what?' she asked, embarrassed.

He lifted a shoulder. 'For being you, I guess.' One hand lifted to push gently through her hair. 'I've been wanting to do that ever since we met...' He broke off, his head tilting towards her.

'That long.' She gave a shaky grin. 'A bit over twenty-four hours ago.'

He lifted his dark eyebrows. 'I could have sworn it was nearer a year. My watch must have stopped.'

'Idiot…'

They sat in silence then, Cate's mind winging backwards as he drew his fingers through hers. You've been down this road before, she reminded herself. But had she? This road with Andrew felt altogether different. Untrammelled.

Closing her eyes, she inhaled the scent of his maleness, stunned to realise that everything about him made her so aware, so finely tuned…

'Cate?' His voice was low, husky.

Cate's heart reacted like a trapped bird against her ribs as he lifted his hands and framed her face, staring down into her eyes for a long moment. Then with a broken little breath that reassured her more than any words could have done, he lowered his mouth to hers.

In a second they had gathered each other in.

Every nerve ending responsive, Cate drank in the feel of his mouth, storing the memory, letting it take away the pain and hurt Rick had inflicted. She didn't want to be hurt again.

Her fingers found their way to the back of his neck, rode the corded muscle, feathered through his dark hair. A convulsive shiver ran through her as his hand found her bare skin, stroked the tautness of her midriff, the underswell of her breast, played down the ridges in her backbone.

Andrew was first to break the exquisite contact. He drew back from her slowly, his breath shallow, his eyes with their tiger-like hunger fixed on her.

Cate felt like a rag doll. Her hands fell to her sides. Turning from him, she got shakily to her feet. She could hardly breathe. Wrapping her arms around her body as if for protection, she looked at him. 'Perhaps you'd better go, Andrew.'

His head bent, he wiped his hands across his eyes. Then in one supple movement he was on his feet and moving to the back of the sofa. His dark head at an angle, he looked at her. 'Why the shock, Cate?'

'We've barely known each other five minutes,' she managed throatily.

He gave her a faintly weary smile. 'Five minutes, five years. What's between us is inevitably going to need a resolution.' And on that comment he left.

Cate waited until she heard the throb of his car engine fade away before she trusted her legs to move. Did he want an affair? With a muffled expletive, she turned her back to the wall and slid down it. More to the point, did *she*?

Cate was full of misgivings as she drove to work on Monday.

She had no idea what to expect from Andrew now. But on the other hand, she admitted with painful honesty, he must be equally in limbo, wondering what reaction he could expect from her. It was a shame she couldn't enlighten him!

By mid-morning she still hadn't seen him, and when one of her patients cancelled she ducked out for a reviving hot drink.

She pushed open the door to the staff-room and found Andrew there. He was standing at the window, staring out, one hand in the side pocket of his jeans, the other nursing a mug of coffee.

'Hello, Cate.'

'Andrew.'

'How're things?' He turned and smiled briefly and her heart jerked in her chest.

Crazy, mixed-up, scary. Take your pick. 'Fine. You?'

'Great.' Who was he kidding? Cate Clifford had got under his guard as no other woman had. But he'd probably wrecked his chances now. He moved to the sink to rinse his mug. 'I'm about to set out on a couple of house calls for Pete.'

Cate forced a smile. 'Got your street directory?'

'You bet. What time do we see your Mrs Twigg?'

Cate stopped in her tracks. She'd completely forgotten. 'I'd rather not leave it too late. She's afraid to open the door after dark.'

Andrew whistled through his teeth. 'Obviously not a good situation.'

'No, not at all. Four o'clock suit you?'

'I'll be ready. Do we need two cars?'

Cate hesitated. She took one look at his long legs and thought of her smallish car. 'Probably not. We can take yours if you like.'

She picked up her coffee and walked past him. As she did, he lifted his hand and caught her wrist gently. 'I think I've found a flat,' he said.

Her breath skittered. 'Is it what you want?'

'It's fine,' he said dismissively. 'There's just one thing I need to check before I take it.'

'Oh?' Unobtrusively Cate reclaimed her wrist. 'Is there a problem?'

'I hope not.' He smiled but it didn't quite reach his eyes. 'It's only one street away from you.'

Wild scenarios juxtaposed in her mind and were dismissed just as quickly. She held his eyes—just. 'It won't be a problem, Andrew. Take it.'

His arms folded, Andrew was standing beside his car when Cate emerged from the surgery just after four.

'Hi,' he said, holding the passenger door open for her.

'Hi,' she echoed, and felt a fluttering inside.

'Looks like the weather's let us down today.'

'Just marginally.' Cate huddled into her red winter coat. In fact, Brisbane's notorious August westerlies had blown up, whipping the last of the winter foliage from the trees and bringing sporadic showers.

'I hope Madeleine's managed to light a fire,' Cate said as he reversed in a swift half-circle and drove out of the car park.

'Surely one of those electric fan heaters would be safer and cleaner?'

Was he inferring she should have done something about her elderly patient's heating? Cate bristled. 'Mrs Twigg has her own way of doing things. I'm not forcing her to change the habits of a lifetime.'

His mouth tightened. 'I take it she does have running water?'

Cate sent her eyes heavenward. Why was he being so moody? 'I take it you know where you're going?'

'I got the address from Chrissie. And I actually did a bit of a Cook's tour this morning after my other calls. Mrs Twigg's house is in the Highgate Hill area, isn't it?'

'Yes.' Cate flexed her toes as the heater warmed the car. 'Parts of the suburbs are quite upmarket but there are still pockets of old family dwellings.'

There was silence as he concentrated on his driving. He didn't need her as a navigator at all, Cate realised, watching the familiar landmarks flash past. 'Did you take the flat?'

He arched an eyebrow. 'I paid them money so I assume I've taken it.'

He sounded so totally uninterested that Cate was forced to wonder again just what made Andrew Whittaker tick. Would she ever find out? Did she want to?

The rain had stopped when they arrived at Madeleine Twigg's house, but the grey clouds still hung perilously low. Cate looked at Andrew as he switched off the engine. 'This is probably not a good time to offer to show Madeleine new accommodation even if she is willing. With the rain and all.'

'Let's just play it by ear. The whole point is to tread softly, I would think.' He seemed on the verge of saying something more, but with an abrupt movement he removed the keys from the ignition and swung out of the car.

Cate had no option but to follow suit. It looked even more dilapidated today, she thought, looking towards Madeleine's old shell of a home—untended, paint peeling, the broken-down front fence held up by decades-old frangipani trees, their rubbery, winter-bare branches like intricate scaffolding.

'Dr Clifford!' A young woman hailed Cate from the open front door of the house.

'Roxanne?' Cate gave a little start. The girl looked agitated. 'What's happened?' she called.

Roxanne made her way down the shallow front steps and out to the car. 'I was just about to ring you.' She cast a scared look at Andrew as he came round from the driver's side. 'Mrs Twigg's not well. I've only just got back...' She took a breath.

'Been away for a week or so. I left some stuff in her fridge but she doesn't seem to have touched it.'

'You go in.' Andrew put a hand on Cate's shoulder. 'I'll get my bag.'

CHAPTER SIX

CATE made a sound of disquiet. Madeleine Twigg looked as though she'd been anchored in the shabby armchair for ever.

Please, God, not a stroke. Cate bent quickly over her elderly patient. Madeleine's head, with its little knot of white hair, was bent forward, her hands clasped together under the blanket covering her knees.

'Madeleine, it's Cate—Dr Clifford. Can you hear me?'

Madeleine Twigg's eyes fluttered open then closed.

'Roxanne!' Cate flung her head up. 'Could you call an ambulance, please? Mrs Twigg will have to go to hospital. And ask them to bring fluids.'

'I'll do it from my place.' The girl ran outside with frightened eyes.

'Febrile?' Andrew had entered unobtrusively and placed his bag on a side table.

'Burning up,' Cate confirmed. 'She's dangerously dehydrated. I'd say she hasn't eaten anything substantial for several days.'

Andrew ran his stethoscope over Madeleine's chest and back. His mouth tightened. 'A few crackles there. Possibly fluid. When did you last see her?'

Cate swallowed. 'It must be over a week ago now.' Cate flinched inwardly. Should she have acted more assertively with Madeleine for the elderly lady's own protection?

'You have to play it as you see it, Cate,' Andrew said quietly. 'Sometimes you win.'

And sometimes you lose. Cate bit her lips together. Would she lose Madeleine?

'The ambulance is on its way.' Roxanne came hurtling through the front door, skidding to a halt. Her hand went to her mouth. 'She's not—?'

'No.' Cate shook her head. 'But she's very ill.'

'Is it my fault?' Roxanne's fingers pleated agitatedly the folds of her long tartan skirt.

'It's no one's fault, Roxanne,' Cate said gently, telling herself to listen to her own advice. She looked across at Andrew. 'This is Dr Whittaker from Ferndale.'

'Oh...' Roxanne's eyes widened. 'I thought you might have been from Social Security or something.'

'I believe you've been a great help to Mrs Twigg,' Andrew said.

Roxanne blushed. 'She's been kind to me.'

'Would you know where Madeleine keeps her night things?' Cate asked with an effort. 'She'll need them for the hospital. And her slippers, sponge bag and whatever else you can think of.'

'I can do that.' The young woman looked eager. 'And I know just where to find everything.'

'Where will you send her?' Andrew asked as they made Madeleine more comfortable.

'I'll see whether St Anne's will take her.' Cate pulled out her mobile phone. 'If they haven't had a lot of admissions to their medical ward today, we might be lucky.'

St Anne's would, indeed, take Madeleine. Cate was just concluding her call when the ambulance arrived. 'Andrew, would you mind doing the necessary?'

'I've examined Mrs Twigg,' Andrew briefed the paramedics. 'She's exhibiting early signs of pneumonia. Slight audible wheeze plus crackles on bases of both lungs. The admitting registrar should X-ray immediately on arrival.'

'Right, Doc, thanks for that.' The officers wheeled the stretcher into place. Very gently, they lifted Madeleine. 'Come on, sweetheart. Easy does it. Now, let's get you to hospital, OK?'

'If you're not pressed for time, I'd like to tidy the house a bit,' Cate said when the ambulance had driven away and they'd walked back inside.

'I'll help you,' Andrew offered promptly. 'Where should we start? Kitchen?'

Cate wrinkled her nose in distaste. 'Poor old lady. Looks like she's been living on tea and toast when she managed to eat anything. You wash. I'll wipe.'

'Yes ma'am.' Andrew gave a mock salute and proceeded to roll up his sleeves.

'This stuff will have to be chucked out,' Cate said, peering into the fridge. 'Check if there are any plastic bags we could use, please, Andrew.'

'At this rate, we'll be able to go into the contract cleaning business,' he said drily some time later. He gave the inside of the refrigerator a last wipe and sent the sponge flying back onto the sink.

'Well, I'd like to leave things halfway decent for when Madeleine comes back.' Cate swiped back a few escaping tendrils of hair with her forearm. 'That's if she comes back,' she added bleakly.

'Cate...' Andrew said warningly. 'You're a dedicated doctor. You could only do as much as your patient would allow you to.'

'I know all that,' she said impatiently. 'But if I'd tried harder to get her re-housed—'

'You did try. Madeleine didn't want to leave her home. And elderly as she is, Cate, she still has rights.'

Cate sighed. 'I know and I'll shut up about it now. Thanks for doing all this, Andrew.'

He lifted a shoulder. 'Not a problem. It helped get rid of my bad mood anyway.'

Cate tilted her head enquiringly. 'Were you in a bad mood?'

'You know I was.' The corners of his mouth curved slightly. He looked around, his eyes checking details. 'Is that all we have to do?'

'Mmm.' Cate bagged some old newspapers and tied the top. 'Roxanne said she'll strip the bed and do whatever else is necessary tomorrow.'

'OK, let's go, then.' He picked up his medical bag and headed for the front door. 'Cate?'

'Just coming,' she said, taking a last look around.

'Are you sure you don't need more time off, Bea?' Cate asked, when they met up in the staffroom next morning.

'Jeff's at home today,' the practice manager explained. 'He's happy to hold the fort. We're keeping Will home from school for the rest of the week to be on the safe side, and Andrew's going to check him over again on Friday.'

'No problems?'

'Not so far. But, oh, Cate, we feel so lucky.'

Cate nodded. Will Harrison's accident could have had far worse repercussions.

Bea took a mouthful of her coffee. 'Did you hear Brent is on the mend, too?'

'Mr Walker rang to tell me,' Cate confirmed. 'Which was very nice of him, seeing they're not patients at Ferndale.'

Bea looked thoughtful. 'We're hoping he'll agree for the boys to spend these few days convalescing together at our place.'

Cate smiled. 'That sounds like a wonderful idea, if you can manage.'

'We'll be fine.' Bea turned to rinse her mug. 'My mum's coming to help out as well.'

Cate looked momentarily bleak. 'It's nice when families stick together, isn't it?'

'You're thinking of poor Mrs Twigg, aren't you?' Bea said quietly.

'Mmm.' Cate looked at her watch. 'And while I've a minute, I must ring St Anne's and see what kind of night our Madeleine has had.'

Cate's first patient for the day was three-year-old Shane Edmunds, who had pushed a peanut into his nostril.

'I just couldn't believe he'd done it.' His mother shook her head. 'Normally we don't allow peanuts anywhere near him, but the little monkey found a nut-block of chocolate my husband and I had been eating while we'd been watching telly last night.'

'And the rest, as they say, is history.' Cate's look was wry. She buzzed Jessica. 'Let's get Shane along to the treatment room, Mrs Edmunds. We'll take a look under some brighter lights.'

'Where do you want him, Doctor?' Mrs Edmunds asked a minute or two later. She clasped the child to her and looked across at the treatment couch.

'We'll keep it all low-key,' Cate explained. 'Perhaps if you could hold Shane on your knee so he feels secure?'

With Jessica's help in restraining the little arms that were all set to protest, Cate was able to peer into the child's nasal passage. The peanut was there and firmly lodged.

Cate considered it could be a tricky procedure. 'I don't want to distress Shane any more than necessary, Mrs Edmunds, so I'll have one shot at removing the blockage. But if I can't, we'll have to send you along to an ear, nose and throat specialist.'

The mother bit her lip, tensing, as Cate applied gentle pressure to the foreign body. As though realising as much depended on him, the little lad stayed remarkably still.

'I have it,' Cate said quietly, drawing the forceps slowly from the child's nostril. With a clink, the peanut landed in the receiving dish.

'It's as big as a pea!' the mother exclaimed.

'Kids will be kids.' Jessica grinned.

'But what if he'd inhaled it?'

'Don't dwell on that possibility.' Cate ruffled the little boy's hair. 'Now, if you'd just hold Shane steady again, I'd like to take a final look to make sure there's been no tissue damage.'

'Do you think boys are more accident-prone than girls?' Cate asked a few minutes later, as she washed her hands and Jessica set the treatment room to rights.

The RN chuckled. 'The goings-on this weekend amongst our own little crew would seem to indicate that. We can only hope the guys get smarter as they get older.'

Cate had no comment about that and she made her way back to her consulting room.

Something didn't add up here. Cate was thoughtful as she removed the blood-pressure cuff from her patient's arm. Elysse Maxelton was a new patient Cate had squeezed in at the end of her morning surgery.

At seventeen years old, the young woman had presented as exceptionally fit, but now at the end of her examination Cate wasn't so sure. Obviously, she was going to have to dig for more detailed information and Elysse was not being terribly forthcoming. 'Tell me about your lifestyle,' Cate encouraged. 'What you do for fun and so on.'

The girl shrugged. 'I exercise a bit.'

'In what form?' Cate enquired, several possibilities for the odd symptoms springing to mind.

'Twice a day at the gym. I run as well.'

'Are you in training for something?'

'No, I'm useless at sports.'

Yet something was driving this young woman to put her body through untold stress. Puzzled, Cate replaced the sphygmomanometer in its metal case. 'Are your periods regular?'

Elysse hesitated. 'I haven't had one for six months. They were always regular before.'

Immediately Cate was alerted. At this rate the young woman was heading towards a condition known as amenorrhoea. 'I'd like you to have a blood test done,' she said practically. 'You could be lacking iron. And we need to discuss your diet.'

Elysse swallowed unevenly. 'What's wrong with me?'

Cate grabbed a scribble block and drew a quick explanatory diagram. 'Your body is responding to the extraordinary physical demands you're placing on it. No periods mean no ovulation and severely reduced hormone levels. I'd encourage you to rethink your lifestyle, Elysse. If you keep on like this, you're leaving yourself open to stress fractures, even osteoporosis.'

Elysse's eyebrows almost touched the tip of her white-blond fringe. 'I thought that only happened to oldies!'

'Far from it.' Cate shook her head. 'If you think of your body as a delicately balanced machine, you'll get the picture. When one part becomes out of kilter, the effects are felt elsewhere. But don't be alarmed.' Cate gave a disarming smile. 'I think we can safely say you've sought help in time. We'll see what the blood test turns up and then I'd like you to have a chat with a dietitian.'

'Do I have to? Couldn't I keep coming to see you?'

'Possibly.' Cate completed the request form for Elysse's blood test. 'We'll talk about it on your next visit. Perhaps you'd like to bring your mum along as well,' Cate added, thinking if changes had to be made in the family's eating patterns a chat with the girl's mother would seem helpful.

'My parents are divorced.' Elysse bit her lip, staring down at the referral note Cate had passed to her. 'I live with my father.'

Suddenly, Cate sensed a bigger problem.

Softly, softly, she cautioned herself inwardly. First, she would have to get her patient's trust and then and only then could she begin to get at the real cause of Elysse's problem.

When her patient had gone, Cate sat on at her desk, her head lowered, her fingers gently massaging her temples.

Had she opened some kind of Pandora's box with Elysse? she wondered. And what kind of relationship did the girl have with her mother? Did she get on with her father?

Cate sighed. Adolescence was a time of upheaval anyway. Add a divorce and you had a teenager in turmoil.

She snorted, considering her own turmoil. Andrew had left her with hardly a word after they'd got back from Madeleine's last night. She hadn't meant to freeze him out, she thought dismally. Only slow things down a bit. Get to know one another. She made a little noise of frustration, suddenly angry at the emotional games people played.

A rap sounded on her door.

'Yes, come in.' Cate hurriedly schooled her expression.

'Got a minute?' Andrew's head came through the opening.

'Several, I should think.' Cate brought her gaze up to meet his.

'Tough morning?'

'No more than usual. Did you want something?'

He folded his arms and looked at her. 'Are you all right?'

'Of course I'm all right,' she said crossly.

'I'll leave if you like.'

Cate pointed to the chair. 'If you want to talk, Andrew, please, sit down,' she said heavily.

He did and for a few moments they sat in awkward silence.

'Sorry.' Cate was the first to break it. 'I didn't mean to snap your head off.'

He shrugged. 'It's OK. Your eyes change to the most amazing shade of topaz when you're tetchy.'

'Please.' Cate felt a bubble of laughter rise in her chest.

'I'm serious.'

'I believe you.' In a nervous action, Cate caught her hair up from her collar and let it go. 'What did you want to see me about?'

'Who, actually. What's the update on Madeleine?'

'I spoke to the registrar this morning. Madeleine does have pneumonia but, thanks to your alert, they've caught it in time. She's on antibiotics now which will probably save her life…'

'Madeleine can't go back to that house, Cate,' Andrew said quietly.

'I know…'

'Is there no family?'

'Madeleine's husband died years ago, apparently. There's an adopted daughter…'

'What's the story?' Andrew's concentration deepened, the lines and grooves in his face showing up in sharp relief.

Cate hesitated. She supposed she wasn't breaking confidentiality. 'It seems the Twiggs hadn't told her. It was Mr Twigg who was against it. When he died, Madeleine thought she should know. After all, she was then a grown woman.'

He arched an eyebrow. 'She didn't take it well?'

Cate shook her head. 'She was angry, bitter. Dropped Madeleine like a stone. Never came back.'

'We could try to trace her.'

'It's been years and years, Andrew.'

'That's nothing.' He slid his hands towards Cate across the desk. 'Do you have her name?'

Cate's brow furrowed. 'Sandra—no—Sylvia!'

Andrew nodded in satisfaction. 'I'll get on to the Salvation Army tracing service. Their success rate in finding people is very high.'

'But she could have a married name now.' Cate looked doubtful.

'That's not insurmountable.'

'Andrew…' Cate dropped her gaze. 'You don't have to do this.'

'Yes, I do.' His hands closed over hers. 'It matters to you, Cate, what happens to Madeleine. So it matters to me.'

Colour stole into her cheeks. 'Even if they find her, it doesn't guarantee a reconciliation,' she pointed out quietly. 'Are we meddling, Andrew?'

'Of course we're not.' He gazed at her levelly. 'The counsellors at the Sally Army are skilled go-betweens. Contact is only possible if both parties agree.' His voice softened persuasively. 'Isn't it worth a try, Cate?'

Cate suddenly had a mental picture of her elderly patient, alone, fragile, vulnerable. Surely at the end of her days she had the right to be surrounded with family. Perhaps there were grandchildren as well. Lifting a hand, Cate toyed with the chain at her throat, waiting for the spasm in her stomach to subside.

She wasn't naïve enough to imagine that establishing contact between the two women would be easy or painless, but achieving it at all—that had to be a plus.

'Well?' Andrew arched an eyebrow. 'Do we start the ball rolling?'

Cate nodded slowly. 'Yes. Let's at least give it a shot.'

'Good.' He squeezed her hand. 'I'll start working the phone this afternoon.'

He drew in his legs, about to stand. Seeing the action, Cate had a compellingly urgent need to keep him there. 'When are you moving into your flat?'

He sank back in his chair, his eyes narrowing. 'In a couple of days. The basics are already there and I've ordered a bed which should be delivered tomorrow.' He made a helpless movement with his hands. 'Despite my protests, Ellie insists in loading me up with linen and kitchen stuff.'

Cate looked at him from under her lashes. 'Can I supply anything?'

He stared at her, then smiled slowly. 'What did you have in mind?'

Her heart missed a beat. His eyes were asking a thousand questions she couldn't begin to find answers to. For the briefest moment she was gripped by confusion then took refuge in humour. 'Oh, I wondered about a candelabra? Lace tablecloth?'

He chuckled. 'Don't think I'll be needing them. Thanks all the same.'

Cate linked her hands in her lap. 'Am I getting an invitation to see it?'

'Come round this afternoon if you like,' he said offhandedly. 'I'm going there after work to check if the electricity has been reconnected.'

'OK.' In a flash Cate decided she could manage that quite nicely. 'We can go back to my place then, and I'll feed you. I've a couple of prime steaks in the fridge.'

'Sounds good,' he murmured, holding her dark eyes with his own brilliant blue gaze. 'Then it'll be my turn to feed you.'

She gave a disbelieving look. 'You can cook?'

'Got a chef's apron to prove it.'

A smile crept slowly over Cate's lips. 'So, if the food's not up to much, at least we get to admire the apron, is that it?'

'Oh, ye of little faith.' An imp of mischief danced in Andrew's eyes. 'In Cambodia, when I wasn't doctoring, I learned to make a pretty mean risotto.'

She grinned, her whole face lighting up

from within. 'I'll look forward to it, then.'

His heart wrenched.

Oh, dear, Cate thought, entering Andrew's flat. The place needed work, beginning with the pale green walls which reminded her of hospital waiting rooms of yesteryear.

'It's all on one level.' Andrew walked her down the short hallway. 'Living room, bedroom, bathroom. Laundry off the kitchen. What do you think?'

'It's OK.'

'But.' Andrew's look was wry.

'Sorry?'

'Your face gives you away every time, Cate.' He spun his arms wide. 'Well, what's wrong with it?'

She looked at him hesitantly. 'Nothing that a coat of white paint wouldn't fix. And here…' She moved quickly back to the entry. 'There's just room for a hall table, nothing too grand. And we could sponge-paint it. And perhaps a brass lamp and a couple of flower prints for the wall. Or, if you didn't fancy that, you could have a chunky bench seat and a peg rail. And plants, Andrew.' She turned back to the empty living room. 'We could go to the nursery—'

'Cate! Stop! You're making me dizzy.'

Startled, she backed against the wall and looked at him. 'You don't like my ideas, do you?'

He shook his head. 'It's not that. I'm just not interested in decorating. This place is a short-term arrangement. That's all.'

Short term so he could up and leave without a backward glance. No roots. No ties. Cate felt pain stab through her. She didn't want him going anywhere. The thought rocked her to the core.

'I'll save my breath, then.' She laughed shakily. 'And it's obvious the power's on.' She looked up to where the lighted bulb hung from the ceiling. 'We may as well make tracks—'

'Cate...' Andrew lifted a hand and rubbed the back of his neck. 'I've upset you and I'm sorry,' he said, his voice tight. 'You're a natural home-maker, and I love your ideas.'

'Do you?' She swallowed, feeling a bit like she'd been handed the thin end of the wedge.

'Of course I do...' He put out a hand, drawing her into his arms.

Cate took a shattered breath, thought about resisting but clung to him instead, absorbing the unique male feel of him, glorying in the absolute rightness of his arms about her.

'Do you feel this, too, Cate? This pull between us?' He lifted her chin, intending only to gauge her reaction. Instead, he found himself stirred beyond belief.

His breath rasped as he cupped her face, his thumbs following the contours of her cheekbones. She looks so vulnerable, he thought, looking down at the little flecks

like gold dust in her eyes. And her skin—
so soft, so fine.

He breathed in, capturing her fragrance,
distinctive, special only to her. This wasn't
supposed to happen. He travelled alone.
With a ragged sigh, his mouth sought hers.

'Sweet,' he murmured, knowing already
that one kiss would never be enough, that
this brief brushing of lips could only fuel
the fire that was waiting to be lit.

He tasted the fluttering pulse at her throat
before catching her lips again, winding his
fingers through her hair to lock her head
more closely to his.

On a little gasp of pleasure Cate wel-
comed his deepening kiss, the interplay of
taste and texture, finding it hard to believe
sensations she hadn't known it was possible
to experience. She hung on tighter, closing
the last gap between them, tasting heaven.

But in a matter of weeks he'd be gone.

With a tiny whimper she dragged her
mouth from his, her breathing erratic.

'Andrew...' She looked at him with dazed, bewildered eyes. 'This is crazy.'

'You want me as much as I want you, Cate.' The words were hoarsely spoken, interrupted by his shallow breathing.

Cate swallowed. 'I don't deny that.'

'Then trust your feelings...'

She skimmed away as he would have drawn her close again. 'You want sex without strings, Andrew.'

His jaw tightened. 'Is that so wrong? We're both adults here.'

'Don't use those old clichés on me, Andrew.' She wound her arms around her midriff to stop herself trembling. 'Anyway...' She licked her lips, tasting him all over again. 'We're totally at odds here. You obviously just take what's on offer at the time.'

He rubbed his hand wearily through his hair. 'You imagine I thrive on one-night stands, do you, Cate?'

She lifted a shoulder, her meaning clear.

'Don't presume to judge how I live my life, Cate.'

Cate's hands were trembling like wind-blown leaves as she bent to retrieve her shoulder-bag from the floor. She felt swamped, out of kilter. Foolish. Why couldn't she be cool around him? She had to get things into perspective. But how could she do that when she couldn't even think straight around him?

'Where are you going?' he demanded as she walked towards the front door.

'Home.' She brought her head up, ignoring the ache that was rapidly forming behind her eyes. 'I've steaks to cook for dinner.'

'Cate, wait a minute.' In a few strides he'd caught her, hauling her back into his arms. For long moments they stood there, his hand stroking the back of her head where it rested against his shoulder. 'Talk to me, Cate.'

There was such gentleness in his voice, such entreaty, she would have had to have been made of ice not to respond. Slowly she raised her head.

'You've been hurt, haven't you?' He lifted a strand of her hair and wound it around his finger.

A long sigh shook her body. 'Haven't we all?'

Andrew's eyes narrowed. 'Is it recent?'

'Fairly. And I don't want to talk about it. OK?' Gently, she disengaged his arms and sent him an artificial smile. 'Now, are we cooking these steaks, Doctor?'

His hands went to his back pockets. 'I'll take a rain check if you don't mind.'

Cate nodded, feeling relief and regret all rolled into one. At the entrance to the hall she turned back and looked at him. He seemed so alone, standing there in the almost empty room.

Her throat constricted.

'What?' he said flatly.

A small smile appeared on Cate's face. 'Just one plant, Andrew? Please?'

His head went back in a laugh of disbelief, and to Cate he suddenly looked ten years younger. 'Just one, then,' he said. 'And it had better be a beauty.'

'It will be.' Cate could still hear his chuckle as she left.

CHAPTER SEVEN

IT WAS only her work that was keeping her sane, Cate thought as she waited for Elysse Maxelton to arrive for her appointment.

It was Friday again, a week since Andrew Whittaker had jumped into her life. A week since he'd taken her emotions on a roller-coaster ride.

She shivered, shoving her wrists under the tap at the basin, willing her pulse to slow down. She hadn't seen him to speak to since the night at his flat, except for some very casual remarks when the rest of the staff had been present.

Had he moved into his flat? She supposed so. She worried about him. He seemed jaded, with the kind of ingrained tiredness she remembered from her years as an intern. Was he not sleeping?

Get out of my head, Andrew! she cried inwardly, mentally dousing herself with cold water. She couldn't ask him to get out of her heart. She knew only too well he was anchored there.

'Come on in, Elysse,' Cate said a little later. Seeking a less confrontational approach, she came from behind her desk and sat beside her young patient. 'How are you today?'

'OK.' Elysse clutched her tote bag, which resembled an over-stuffed cushion, close to her chest. She looked at Cate warily. 'Do you have my blood test back?'

'Yes, and it shows you're anaemic. I can prescribe you an iron preparation which you'll need to stay on until your haemoglobin level returns to normal.'

'How long?'

'Several months probably,' Cate said. 'Then we'll test you again to see if your iron stores have been filled.'

Elysse's shoulders slumped in relief. 'I thought I had something awful,' she confessed, 'when I told you about being dizzy and stuff. But if I take the medicine, I should be OK, shouldn't I?'

If only it were that simple, Cate thought.

'There's a lot more involved than just taking medicine, Elysse,' she said carefully. 'You're going to have to cut back your exercise to a lower level for starters. And you're still growing. You need to be eating the right foods. What kinds of meals do you normally eat? For instance, dinner at night?'

'Dad brings home take-aways.' The girl's arms tightened around her tote bag. 'I don't eat them. I don't want to get fat like Mum.'

'Where is your mother, Elysse? Do you see her?' Cate was loath to pry but the youngster's health and well-being were at stake.

Elysse lifted a shoulder dismissively. 'She moved to the coast. We don't hit it off.'

'Sometimes that's pretty normal for mother-daughter relationships at your age. As you get older you may find it will change and become better.'

The girl raised stricken eyes. 'My parents never got along. I think they only got married 'cos Mum was pregnant with me...' She swallowed. 'Dad used to nag her about being fat. It's no wonder she left.'

Cate got to her feet. Elysse needed a few seconds to compose herself. Cate filled a glass from the nearby cooler and handed it to her patient. 'Do you and your dad get on?'

'He's OK. Sometimes we go to a movie together. But he hasn't got a clue about running the house. It's all down to me.'

Cate sat quietly. This young person's need to unload had to be accommodated. And the more information Cate had, the better and more accurate her treatment of her patient could be.

Elysse lifted the glass and took a mouthful of water. 'I left school a month ago.'

'Why was that?'

'I didn't fit in. I hated all that stuff. I want to go to work, have a job. I'd like to be a hairdresser. I know I'd be good at it.'

It was the first gleam of positive thinking Elysse had shown, and Cate decided to build on it. 'I think there are ways and means we could find out about an apprenticeship. What about your careers advisor at school?'

'Maybe.'

'Whatever,' Cate said, deciding it was time to become practical, 'you need support from somewhere. Do you have an aunt, perhaps? Grandmother?'

The girl's face brightened. 'I see my gran sometimes. She's OK.' She bit back a smile. 'She's Dad's mother. Usually tears a strip off him for not doing more around the house.'

Instinct told Cate her young patient would have an ally there. In a flash she decided. 'Right, Elysse. I'm going to phone your gran and the three of us are going to have a chat about how we can begin to make life a lot happier for you.'

Elysse shook her head. 'I don't see how—'

'You'll see.' Cate smiled. 'And once your iron preparation starts kicking in and we add lots of fabulous food to your diet, you'll feel like taking on anything. I promise you.'

'Do you like smoothies?' Cate looked across at the youngster, reading the desperate need in her eyes.

Elysse nodded and then a reluctant smile edged her mouth. 'That's milk and bananas whipped together, isn't it?'

'Or whatever fruit turns you on.' Cate grinned. 'Personally, I like passion-fruit or strawberries. Throw in a scoop of ice cream, too, if you like, and nutmeg, wheat-germ.'

'It...sounds lovely.'

Oh, you poor little pet. Cate blinked, wanting to hug the child and take away the hurt and neglect but, of course, she couldn't be so unprofessional. Instead, she picked up the phone. 'Would your gran be home now, Elysse?'

The girl looked startled. 'Are you going to ask her to come here?'

'No,' Cate said quietly. 'We'll go to see her. I've an hour or so before I need to be back here for a staff meeting. So, if you'll give me her phone number, Elysse, I'll ring and tell her to expect us. Is that OK?'

Elysse's quick nod said it all.

'So that's what I've done,' Cate concluded. It was near the end of the staff meeting and she looked hesitantly around the rest of the team.

'Sounds like community medicine at its best,' Jon said approvingly. 'Well done, Cate.'

Andrew looked thoughtful. 'You're not thinking of approaching Mr Maxelton at this stage?'

'I'd prefer the family to try to resolve matters between themselves. But when I next see Elysse I'll be able to better judge how it's all working out.'

Peter looked at Cate over the top of his glasses. 'You're quite certain the grand-mother will keep her word, support the youngster?'

'Right down to accompanying Elysse on a weekly shop and planning the meals. Maisie Maxelton is genuine. I'd stake my reputation on it.' Cate smiled. 'And she's had a real brainwave, too. She's going to encourage Elysse to get her driver's licence. Apparently, Maisie has a little car she no longer uses, which would be ideal for their trips to the supermarket and especially useful if Elysse can get a job.'

'Excellent.' Peter nodded. 'And I can only reiterate Jon's reaction, Cate. Well done.'

'Hear, hear,' Andrew said quietly.

'Well, it just kind of presented as the right thing to do at the time.' Cate felt unexpectedly warmed by her colleagues' approval. And we all need it, she thought—approval. She looked fleetingly at Andrew but he seemed lost in his own thoughts, making meaningless doodles on the pad in front of him.

'If that's it, then, I'm out of here.' Jon got slowly to his feet. 'Everyone set for the party tomorrow?' He sent an enquiring look around the table. At the general murmur of agreement, he grinned, his bright blue gaze homing in on Andrew and Cate. 'As for you two singles, please, feel free to bring a friend.'

Cate tensed. 'Thanks, Jon. But I'll just bring myself.'

Andrew's eyes locked with hers and for an endless moment they stared at each other. Then, with an almost imperceptible lift of his shoulder, he went back to his doodling.

Cate found she could breathe again. 'I'll give Claire a ring to see if she'd like a hand with anything.'

'I'm sure she'd appreciate it.' Jon grinned. 'At only just three, Mitch isn't a great lot of help. We're having a barbecue,' he said. 'I hope that meets with everyone's approval.'

'Well, I must confess it meets with mine.' Peter looked sheepish. 'You all know Ellie and I would much prefer a family gathering where people can bring their kids.'

'And you can have a reasonably early night at the same time.' Andrew exchanged a wry look with his uncle.

Peter chuckled. 'That, too. So, Jon, what time do you and Claire want us?'

Jon Goodsir shrugged. 'Fivish for drinks and nibbles? Then I can start cooking around six.'

With a general consensus the meeting broke up and the four dispersed.

'Cate?'

Cate stopped and half turned as Andrew caught up with her in the corridor.

'We could go together tomorrow evening,' he said. 'Why take two cars?'

Cate blinked. His look was intense. 'I'm on call, Andrew. I'll need my own car.'

His hands went to his hips. 'I wouldn't mind driving you if you get called out.'

For a moment she was tempted and then sanity prevailed. 'I...wouldn't want to take you away from the party.'

'You don't have to keep avoiding me, Cate.'

She swallowed. 'I'm not.'

'Aren't you?'

The air was suddenly thick with tension.

'We've unfinished business, Cate,' he reminded her softly. 'It won't just go away because you want it to.'

Goaded, she brought her chin up. 'Tell me, Andrew. What is it *you* want?'

'Just use your imagination,' he said with a slightly grim smile. 'That should tell you what I want.'

Watching him walk away, his long legs eating up the carpeted space in quick strides, Cate felt the slow build-up of heat inside her.

If he'd been going for shock value, he'd succeeded. She gave a restive little shake of her head, her mind conjuring up a vivid image to match his words.

So what was holding her back? Cate scurried back to her room, as if she were being pursued. The physical attraction between them had the irresistible force of a magnet.

She put a hand to her heart, feeling the crazy fluttering his words had produced. But once before she'd mistaken symbols for substance. Was it any different this time?

But *Andrew* was different. Her every instinct was screaming that. As different from Rick as night was from day.

Cate sprang out of bed on Saturday morning feeling as though she'd reached some kind of watershed. However, if someone had asked her to explain it, she knew she wouldn't have been able to.

But it was there in the form of a new kind of confidence, a feeling of direction.

Her mind was buzzing with things to be done, the least of which was a trip to the supermarket. If she left now, she'd beat the Saturday queues.

In her bedroom she threw on comfortable jeans, a red-and-white-striped jersey and trainers, ran a brush through her hair and slicked on lipstick. Within a few minutes she was reversing her Polo from her garage and heading to the shops.

At the supermarket Cate made her selections quickly and methodically. Coming out of the fruit and vegetable section, she paused, her eyes drawn to a sign advertising a special offer on house plants.

Well, was this or was this not a sign from heaven? Without waiting to consider the possible repercussions from a certain quarter, she made her way across to the display.

Cate knocked on Andrew's front door and waited, her heart banging like a drum inside her chest.

For a split second she considered taking off. Then she heard movement from inside and the door was opening and he was standing there. He was barefoot, a navy blue towelling robe seemingly his only covering.

Cate's heartbeat tripped and threatened to choke her. 'Hi.'

Andrew stared at her blankly for a second and then started to laugh. 'You don't believe in doing things by halves, do you, Cate?'

'Like it?' Proudly, she looked down at the velvety leaves of the plant, its branches taking up most of the stair space beside her.

He rubbed a hand across the dark shadow on his jaw. 'How on earth did you get it here?'

'I left the lid of my boot open. I didn't have far to come, only from the shopping centre.'

'It must weigh a ton,' he said, pretending to stagger as he hefted the ceramic pot and brought it inside.

'It's a ficus,' Cate enlightened him, following hesitantly. 'I thought it might double as a Christmas tree later...'

'Don't even go there, Cate.' His voice was strange, flat and yet somehow expressive.

So nothing had changed. Cate felt her new confidence falter. She bit down on her bottom lip and turned her attention quickly to practical matters.

'You can't stand there holding it all day, Andrew. Where would you like to put it?'

'Don't ask,' he growled.

'Don't be pathetic.' Cate twirled slowly. 'Over here, I think, near the archway. Then you'll see it when you come in and it'll remind you to water it.'

'Like how?' He gave a dry laugh. 'In tree-talk?'

Cate rolled her eyes. 'Grouchy this morning, aren't we, Doctor?'

She watched as he placed the plant on the floorboards, his movements a bit jerky and strained. She brought a hand up to her throat. Had she done the right thing in coming here this morning?

'Coffee?' He shot her a quick enquiring look and walked off to the kitchen.

Cate followed, her knees oddly shaky.

'You're out and about early,' he said.

'Mmm.' Cate watched him as he filled the kettle and plugged it in, then stood looking out of the window at the neat back gardens along the street.

'Thanks for the plant,' he said eventually, and his voice sounded back to its normal pitch, resonant, confident.

Cate breathed a sigh of relief and thanked heaven for small mercies. 'There's a card attached that tells you how to look after it,' she said. 'And ficus does pretty well indoors. But they're big feeders.'

Andrew looked blank.

'Sorry.' Cate suppressed a giggle. 'I mean they like plant food quite often. A slow-release fertiliser is best. I've a huge bag at home. I'll let you have some.'

'With instructions, please.' He switched off the power and made the coffee. 'Would you like something to go with this? I've raisin bread, I think.'

'No, thanks.' Cate shook her head. 'But you go ahead.'

'I'll pass,' he said, opening the fridge and getting out a carton of milk. He placed it beside her mug of coffee. 'I'll make an omelette later when I've had a shower and cleaned up a bit.' He rubbed ruefully at the new growth of beard on his jaw.

Cate took a mouthful of coffee. They were seated on high stools beside one another at the breakfast bar. 'Are you going to buy a setting for the dining alcove?'

He shot her a fleeting grin. 'That's taking comfort a bit far, wouldn't you say?'

'Andrew!' She said his name on a howl of frustration.

His mouth curved into a lazy smile. 'I'm kidding, Cate. And you react so beautifully.'

She glared at him. 'I don't know why I bother.'

'Don't you?' he murmured.

Cate took a shallow breath, felt the tingle of awareness down her spine. 'Did you get your bed?' She cringed inwardly. What on earth had possessed her to ask that?

'Of course...' His voice was low, throaty. 'Like to try it out with me?'

Desperately. 'Not just now. In fact...' she glanced at her watch '...I should be gone.'

'I want you,' he said deliberately.

Cate's eyes glazed.

'Lovers, Cate. You and me...'

She licked her lips, feeling the agonisingly pleasurable ache at the core of her body. 'Andrew...'

He gave her a lopsided smile, his hand on her cheek. 'For you, I'd even shave.'

She lowered her gaze to blot out the tenderness in his eyes, taking a breath so deep it hurt.

'Lovers, Cate,' he whispered. 'Picture it...'

'Andrew...'

'I'm listening.'

She kept her eyes lowered, unwilling to let him see her fears, her vulnerability. 'Soon.'

He took her hand, slowly separating her fingers and placing her palm against his mouth. 'How soon is soon?'

The gesture disarmed her, brought her very close to the edge. 'Soon,' she repeated unsteadily, extricating her hand. She swallowed heavily. 'What...are your plans for today?'

Andrew picked up his coffee and sipped it slowly. 'I promised to give Jon a hand later, arranging the outdoor furniture and whatever else needs doing for the party.'

'I'll probably see you over there, then. I'm helping Claire with the food preparations. Thanks for the coffee.' She swung jerkily off her stool.

'I'll walk you out,' he said.

Cate left, wondering how her legs could possibly still be carrying her.

For a long time after she'd gone, Andrew remained standing by the door, the impression of her warm body still on him.

He shook his head, as if impatient with his wayward thoughts. 'Give me a break,' he muttered, making his way to the bathroom to shower and shave.

Was her life spiralling out of control? It certainly felt like it. Cate choked back a snort of disbelief. She could hardly remember driving home!

Like a robot, she began unloading her groceries, sorting them into her pantry and refrigerator. A slow-burning heat coursed through her as the memory of his muscular body holding her close became three-dimensional in her mind.

Andrew.

She came slowly back to reality, blinking unseeingly at the jar of coffee in her hand. Was this what falling in love felt like? If it was, then it resembled nothing like she'd experienced with Rick. Nothing at all.

When her mobile phone rang, she took a steadying breath and stepped back into reality.

The call was from one of Cate's patients, Jane Rossiter. She was the mother of four young children and her husband often had to work away from home.

'I don't like to bother you, Dr Clifford,' the anxious mother said, 'but Kirsty's been restless all night, and this morning I noticed little red bumps have broken out on her chest. I suppose I could be fussing unnecessarily—'

'No, Mrs Rossiter.' Cate was firm. 'I'll come. See you in a bit.'

Cate grabbed her case and made her way out to her car, mindful of the fact that no symptoms could automatically be taken for granted. Especially now that several cases of a virulent strain of staphylococcus had recently been diagnosed in children attending local preschool centres.

This particular type of bacteria was a potential killer and medical treatment had to be undertaken without delay. Cate edged her speed up a fraction.

Jane met Cate at the door and apologised again.

'Jane, I'm on call this weekend anyway,' Cate said with a smile. 'And it's not as though I've had to drive twenty miles, is it?'

'No, I suppose not.' The young mother looked wry. 'Come through.' She led Cate along the hallway to the children's bedroom.

'Hi, Kirsty,' Cate said gently, putting her case down beside the bed. 'Mummy tells me you're feeling sick.'

'A bit.' The six-year-old nodded. 'And I'm all hot and scratchy.' She rucked up her nightie to show Cate the spots on her chest.

'Mmm, I see,' Cate said seriously. 'Let's have a good look at you, shall we?' Cate made her examination carefully, relieved to diagnose nothing more potentially serious than chickenpox.

'You've got chickenpox, sweetie,' she said, straightening Kirsty's nightie again. 'No school until the spots have gone, OK?'

'I suppose the other kids will get it as a matter of course,' Jane said ruefully, combing back Kirsty's fair hair with her fingers.

'Quite possibly, but it's probably quite a good thing to get it over with. It can be debilitating to get chickenpox as an adult.' Cate smiled wryly. 'I got it when I was fifteen. It was in the school summer holidays. And I remember going dotty with the itching.'

Jane grinned. 'So, is it still calamine lotion for that?'

'No, actually.' Cate slid open her bag. 'We've something new on the market. I've a sample here somewhere. Here we are—

Solugel. It's supposed to be effective. I'll leave this one with you but it's available without prescription anyway.'

'Thanks, Doctor,' Jane took the tube. 'Luckily, Wayne's home for a couple of weeks just now so he'll be able to give me a hand.'

'That's good.' Cate pressed Kirsty's small hand and got to her feet. 'And the others may not get it.'

'Oh, well.' The mother sounded philosophical. 'We'll just have to wait and see, I guess.'

They walked out together.

'You could pop Kirsty under a warm shower as well,' Cate said. 'Just dab her skin dry with a soft towel and then apply the gel to the spots. A general freshen-up should make her feel much happier. Lots of fluids are essential and small, light meals whenever she wants them. She'll let you know when she feels like getting up and about again.'

'You've put my mind at rest,' Jane said gratefully. 'Thank you so much for coming.'

Cate smiled. 'You're welcome. And call me any time if you've any concerns about Kirsty.'

Glancing at her watch, Cate raised her eyebrows. The morning had simply flown. She'd just have time for a quick sandwich, before heading over to the Goodsirs'.

'That's the green salads done.' Cate firmed the cling wrap over the last bowl and placed it in the fridge.

'Thanks, Cate, that's brilliant.' Claire straightened from a lower cupboard, her face breaking into a satisfied smile. 'That just about does it, I think. Bea's bringing one of her famous mushroom and capsicum salads to go with the steaks and Andrew's given me a recipe for a potato salad with a *difference*.'

'So he really can cook?'

Claire gave a low chuckle. 'I'd bet our Dr Whittaker could do most anything he put his mind to.'

Cate sank onto a kitchen stool. 'He told me he's coming over to give Jon a hand with things.'

'He's been and gone,' Claire said airily.

'Oh.' Cate was suddenly unsettled. Had Andrew meant to avoid her deliberately? He'd seemed to want just the opposite this morning. She felt her skin warm at the thought as she watched Claire pour boiling water into the teapot.

'I think we've earned this.' Claire poured the freshly brewed tea. 'It'll be fun catching up with everyone this evening, won't it?'

'Mmm.' Cate nodded her enthusiastic agreement.

'I've invited my friend, Lyn Scali,' Claire confessed with a conspiratorial little smile. 'I figure she and Andrew might be good for each other. Lyn's done a couple of overseas tours for Care Australia,' she went on. 'That experience should at least give them something in common.'

Cate froze, swallowing the words that threatened to fall from her tongue. That she and Andrew were—

Were what?

Biting the inside of her bottom lip, she looked down at the tea in her mug as if trying to find an answer, but there was no inspiration to be found. Instead, she felt enveloped in a great sea of uncertainty, paddling wildly and getting nowhere.

'Is he settling in?' Claire asked.

Cate held back grim laughter. As much as he intends to. 'It's a bit early to tell really. Claire…' Cate rose quickly to her feet. 'I'll have to dash, if you don't mind. Couple of hospital visits to make,' she invented. 'I'll see myself out.'

CHAPTER EIGHT

EVEN soaking in a lavender-scented bath failed to ease Cate's strained nerves. Her mouth twisted wryly as she toyed with the idea of simply not attending the party at all. But that was impossible. The Maguires were special people.

Driven to make the most of her appearance for reasons she wasn't about to analyse, she went through her wardrobe systematically.

Obvious party-type garments presented themselves but were rejected. Of course, she was tempted to dress to the nines but foremost in her mind was the fact she was on call.

She made a compromise somewhere in between and pulled on black evening trousers and a silk shirt in softest gold. She used a minimum of make-up, deciding to emphasise only her eyes, smoothing on shadow to add depth and mascara to accent her lashes.

Why was she even bothering? Cate made a face at her reflection in the dressing-table mirror as she slid gold hoops through her ears. Because, like it or not, she now seemed to have to compete with Lyn Scali for Andrew's attention.

Cate was almost at her car when her mobile rang, the call directing her to Terence Walsh. Mr Walsh, one of Peter's patients, was in his seventies and lived alone. Cate was there within minutes.

'I feel a right old duffer,' he lamented. 'I went to take my Lasix and found I was clean out. And not only that—my prescription's expired.'

Immediately Cate could sense the elderly man was seeing it all as something of a crisis and becoming agitated in the process of recounting the facts.

'It's not a problem, Mr Walsh.' She sat beside him on the lounge. 'I can let you have enough medication to see you over the weekend and I'll write you a new script you can have filled on Monday. How does that sound?'

He nodded his white head. 'That sounds all right to me, lass. But I should've remembered to tie it all up with Dr Maguire before he left. Who will see me now when I come to the surgery?'

Cate knew Peter had prepared his patients for his forthcoming absence, advising them that they would in future see Andrew. It seemed obvious that Mr Walsh had already become confused and simply forgotten.

'You'll see Dr Whittaker now, Mr Walsh,' Cate said, taking down details of the medication from the script duplicate.

Terence Walsh pulled his cardigan more firmly around his thin shoulders. 'Young whippersnapper, is he?'

'No, I wouldn't say that.' Cate bit back a smile. 'Dr Whittaker is a former army medical officer with lots of experience.'

'Might be all right, then, I s'pose,' the elderly gentleman conceded.

As a result of having to attend to Mr Walsh's needs, Cate arrived later than the other guests. As she was on call, Jon had arranged to leave a space in his carport for her Polo.

Just as well, Cate thought ruefully, seeing the line of cars already parked along the street. Pocketing her keys, she made her way towards the music and laughter emanating from the rear garden of the Goodsirs' ranch-style home.

Ellie Maguire greeted her with a warm hug. 'It's been too long.' She smiled. 'And it'll be much longer again before we see you all, I suppose.'

Returning the hug, Cate said lightly, 'Just make sure you enjoy every moment of your holiday.' Marc, the elder of the Harrison boys, appeared with a tray of drinks and Cate selected a fruit juice. Lifting the glass, she took a careful swallow, every nerve honed as she looked around for Andrew.

She saw him almost immediately in close conversation with Lyn Scali. Well, what did you expect? a little voice said in her head.

Cate's expression clouded. Lyn was obviously making a statement, the plain, straight-cut black dress emphasising her elegant slenderness. Her make-up was dramatic, calling attention to her high cheekbones and large eyes as she lifted her face to Andrew's.

Cate's fingers clenched on her glass. For a wild moment she considered staking her claim, marching across the lawn and—

'Make a striking couple, don't they?' Ellie Maguire said, her gaze following Cate's. 'How do you think my nephew is settling back into civilian life?'

He doesn't confide in me! Cate wanted to shriek. He only asked me to sleep with him. 'He's a grown man, Ellie. I expect he made a considered choice.'

The older woman shook her head. 'I worry about him, though.'

'About me?' Peter appeared at his wife's side and slung an arm affectionately around her shoulders.

'Certainly not.' Ellie nudged him playfully in the ribs. 'Cate and I were just talking about Andrew and how he's settling down.'

Peter shrugged. 'Seems OK to me. What's your opinion, Cate?'

'I think he's very much his own person.' The words came out with difficulty. Her mouth—in fact, all her facial muscles—felt stiff with the effort of keeping her expression under control.

There was the tiniest awkward silence until Peter deftly closed the gap. 'Ah.' He looked towards the barbecue. 'Looks like

Jon's calling us to eat. The steaks smell marvellous, don't they?'

'You go ahead, then.' Cate dredged up a smile. 'I must have a word with Bea.'

As an excuse it was the best she could do. Turning, she stared at Andrew's back, her face pale, her eyes unduly dark. 'Oh, hell,' she whispered raggedly, recognising the great hard lump in her chest for what it was. Pure, unadulterated jealousy.

Cate licked her lips. She felt almost afraid of the intensity of her feelings. She brought her head up, absorbing her surroundings as if to regain some semblance of reality.

Jon and Claire had gone to a great deal of trouble to create a party atmosphere. And it was all so lovely. The round tables were covered with white cloths and decorated with trailing green leaves. There was wine in stone coolers and a long serving table literally groaning with food to accompany the barbecued steaks.

She looked upwards to where the stars were splashed across the night sky and realised she'd never felt so alone in her life.

Out of the corner of her eye, she watched Andrew get chairs for Lyn and himself. She watched him drop easily into the wicker seat, a leg crossed so one ankle rested on his opposite knee. As Cate watched, he threw back his head, laughing at something Lyn had said.

Damn him, Cate thought in swift fury. She turned away convulsively, making her way across to Bea and her husband as they toasted themselves beside one of the small braziers. She greeted them, her smile brittle. 'Mind if I join you?'

Cate hardly knew how she got through the next few minutes. But she did know her conversation was too forced, her smile too bright.

'Can I get you another drink, Cate?' Jeff Harrison got to his feet and collected their glasses. 'Perhaps you'd like wine this time?'

'Nothing for me, thanks, Jeff,' she said with an effort. 'I'm on call.'

'Drew the short straw, did you?'

'It might be an idea if we eat, then,' Bea came in. 'While your luck's holding.'

Cate felt food would choke her but she had no will to do anything but go along with Bea's suggestion.

They ate in silence for a while, until Cate said, 'I haven't seen Will about.'

'He didn't come with us,' Bea explained. 'Opted to stay overnight with Brent and his dad.'

'Andrew's given him a clean bill of health, though,' Jeff chimed in. 'School on Monday.'

Bea chuckled. 'I imagine the little monkey will dine out on the story for all he's worth.'

Cate held herself tightly. It seemed that wherever she went, whomever she spoke to,

Andrew's name came up over and over. Lifting her hand, she rubbed at the ache forming behind her temple.

When Chrissie and Jessica arrived with their boyfriends and joined them, Cate was beginning to feel like a fifth wheel, slightly desperate and the odd one out.

Would she ever pick the right man? Her thoughts were starkly honest. She'd be thirty in a couple of months and her biological clock was telling her she needed a mate, a shared life, children...

'Oh, there's Andrew!' Chrissie waved. 'He's seen us. Looks like he's coming over.'

Panicked, Cate pushed her chair back awkwardly. 'I think I'll get a coffee.' Feeling as though every eye was on her, she picked her way quickly across to the serving table.

'Cate?'

She turned. Andrew was so close she could see the fine lines beside his eyes and bracketing his mouth. A snatch of masculine cologne caught her nostrils as she took a shaken breath.

'I didn't see you arrive,' he said. 'Why didn't you come and say hello?' To Cate's stretched nerves it sounded like an accusation of some kind.

'I was late. I had to make a house call. You seemed very content where you were, anyway. I didn't like to interrupt.'

'That was a bit juvenile, wasn't it?' His comment was dry and unamused.

'Do you want a coffee?' she asked abruptly.

'No.' He looked narrowly into her eyes. 'I think we should talk.'

'Talk?' She stared at him. 'I've had the impression that was the last thing on your agenda, Andrew.'

A nerve worked in his jaw and he folded his arms. 'We don't seem to be giving each other much comfort at all, do we, Cate?'

She had no answer to that. Her heart began beating sickeningly fast, exacerbating her feeling of drowning in his closeness.

It seemed providential when her mobile rang.

She stepped inside onto the sheltered verandah to take the call, unsurprised to find him still waiting when she came back. 'I have to go,' she said crisply.

'Urgent?'

Cate moved her hands restlessly. 'Kurt Hayward.'

'The father of the child with leukaemia.'

Cate nodded. 'His wife, Ginny, is in some distress. Apparently, it's all just hit her. She's been crying for hours.' She looked at him distractedly. 'I'll just tell Jon I'm leaving.'

'I'll wait for you,' Andrew said firmly. 'Walk you out to your car.'

'There's no need,' she protested weakly. 'I'm just in the carport.'

Then she realised she might as well have saved her breath.

Cate swore silently as she tried again to start the car and again it failed to respond. 'Damn!' she snarled, looking up, tight-lipped, when Andrew rapped on her window. She wound it down.

'It sounds like your battery's packed in,' he said. 'I'll drive you.'

'I'll get a cab.' Hefting her bag, Cate threw herself out of the driver's seat.

'Don't mess about, Cate.' He began propelling her towards the street where his Audi was parked. 'It's Saturday night,' he emphasised. 'You'll be hanging about for ages.'

Cate gave in. He was probably right and she was desperately concerned about Ginny Hayward's state of mind.

'It sounds like a clear case of anxiety and depression as a result of the diagnosis,' Andrew said as they drove.

'Yes.'　Cate's　heart　wrenched. Apprehensively, she looked across at his stern profile, and said quietly, 'I appreciate this, Andrew.'

He spun her a fleeting look. 'It's a team effort, Cate. We both agreed to give the Haywards our support, as I recall.'

Cate's shoulders lifted in a shrug.

It was a twenty-minute drive to the Haywards' housing commission flat. Cate chewed her bottom lip. She and Andrew could make their journey in silence or ease the tension and talk. She decided on the latter.

'Any word from the Salvation Army tracing service?'

'They've told me they're making progress,' he said. 'I'm sorry I don't actually know what that means. What's happening with Madeleine?'

'She's picked up quite well and been moved to a side ward to convalesce. But, of course, the hospital can't keep her indefinitely.'

Andrew's gaze narrowed on the traffic ahead. 'You haven't spoken to her about moving to a retirement complex, I take it?'

'I was waiting for her health to improve before I said anything. I'll speak to her next week.'

'My offer still stands, Cate.'

'About coming with me to see her?'

'If she's up to it, we could make it a bit of an outing for her. See the home and perhaps have afternoon tea somewhere. Create a new link with the outside world for an old lady.'

Cate gave a wry smile. 'Next you'll be suggesting we invite Roxanne along for the ride as well.'

'Why not, if you think it will help? Nothing gets resolved if you don't work at it, Cate.'

Cate swallowed. Why did she get the impression he was referring to something else entirely? 'It's the next street on the right for the Haywards',' she said.

'Would you like me to come in with you?' Andrew asked, as he pulled into the kerb and cut the engine.

Cate felt relief sweep through her. She hadn't been looking forward to this at all. 'If you wouldn't mind.'

Kurt met them at the door, and immediately Cate felt herself absorbing some of his anxiety. His eyes were bloodshot, his hair every which way, as though he'd spent hours in anguish.

She made the introductions quickly and added, 'My car wouldn't start so Dr Whittaker kindly gave me a lift.'

Kurt nodded absently, as if the matter of how she'd got there was neither here nor there. He just seemed overwhelmingly grateful to see them there at all.

'I don't know what to do,' he said bleakly. 'Ginny's been a tower of strength since Shannon was hospitalised. But now…' He shook his head.

'Has Ginny been staying overnight at the hospital?' Cate asked gently.

He nodded. 'Until today. We got home about four o'clock this afternoon and she just collapsed in tears and couldn't stop.'

Andrew reached out a hand and placed it on the man's shoulder. 'Where is your wife now, Mr Hayward?'

'In the lounge room. She's just lying there. It's like her heart's breaking—'

'Is your other daughter here?' Cate cut in, wondering if perhaps they would have to deal with an over-anxious sibling as well.

'My folks have taken her for the weekend.'

'Right,' Cate said. 'I'll pop in and see Ginny now.' Her eyes sought Andrew's with a plea.

He nodded. 'How about you and I rustle up some tea, Kurt? I'm sure we could all do with a cup.'

'Oh, yeah. Sure, Doc.' He seemed grateful to have something positive to contribute. 'Kitchen's this way.'

'I couldn't help noticing the stained-glass panels in your front door,' Andrew was saying as he followed Kurt along the hallway. 'They're very effective, aren't they?'

'Did them myself.' Kurt sounded pleased. 'It's a hobby of mine.'

Well done, Andrew. Cate's heart lifted slightly. The Haywards' lounge room was small and neat, softly lit by a standard lamp in the corner.

'Ginny?' Cate touched a hand to the shoulder of the woman's huddled form. 'It's Cate Clifford.'

The young mother's eyes flew open and she struggled to sit up. 'Has something—?'

'No! No.' Cate lowered herself onto the edge of the lounge. 'Kurt called me. He's very concerned about you.'

Ginny sank back against the cushions, her breath coming out in a long ragged sigh. 'I...don't know what happened. We got home from seeing Shannon and—' Fresh tears began springing from her eyes. She sniffed determinedly. 'I meant to be the strong one...'

'What you're feeling is a pretty normal reaction to Shannon's diagnosis.' Cate opened her bag. 'I'm going to give you something to help you relax and then we'll talk if you'd like to.'

Cate quietly left the lounge room and went to the kitchen for water.

'How is she, Dr Clifford?' Kurt pushed his chair back from the table and bounced to his feet.

'She appears quite exhausted, Kurt. And I get the impression she's been feeling like she has to carry the entire load for the family.' Cate didn't mince her words. 'I'm about to give her a sedative. I wonder if you'd get me a glass of water, please?'

'What will you give her?' Andrew asked quietly. 'Valium?'

Cate nodded. 'It's called for, I think. But only five milligrams.'

Kurt handed Cate the water. 'Could I see my wife, Dr Clifford? I...never thought...I mean, I thought I was helping.'

Andrew got to his feet. 'Perhaps it's time for a frank discussion about things. Kurt, why don't you bring the tea through and Dr Clifford and I will try to answer any questions you have about Shannon's illness?'

It was almost an hour later when Cate and Andrew were ready to leave.

'So, you think there's a good chance our little girl will lick this?' Kurt held his wife's hand and relief was showing in both their faces.

'We can't deal in certainties,' Andrew said patiently for the umpteenth time, 'but, according to Jon's report, the first chemo went well, as I'm sure he's told you.'

The parents nodded. 'She wasn't as sick as they warned us she might be,' Ginny said.

'And she's a fighter.' Kurt squeezed his wife's hand. 'Like her mum.'

'Well, you should hang onto that.' Andrew stood, gesturing to Cate to do the same. 'Do we have some sleeping pills with us, Dr Clifford?'

Cate nodded. She'd been about to suggest the same thing. Taking the supply of temazepam from her bag, she doled out a single tablet and left it on the tray. 'That should give you a good night's sleep, Ginny.' She smiled. 'And perhaps a warm bath also might be beneficial.'

'And we're only as far away as the surgery if you need to talk to any of us again,' Andrew offered graciously.

They took their leave and Cate sat quietly in the car absorbing her impressions. 'Do you think they'll cope?' she asked.

'Hell, Cate.' Andrew twisted the ignition key almost viciously. 'Ask me something easy.'

Feeling rebuffed, Cate wound her arms around herself in a gesture of self-preservation. What a dreadful evening it had turned out to be! She felt exhausted, as if she'd been put through a wringer not once but several times. 'Could you drop me at home, please?'

'Not going back to the party?'

'No. I'll phone the Maguires in the morning before they leave.'

'What do you want to do about your car?'

Cate wound her arms more tightly around her. 'I'll get on to my motoring club first thing. If I arrange to meet them over at the Goodsirs', they should be able to fit a replacement battery for me promptly.'

Andrew slowed for a light change. 'What if you're called out again?'

'I'll get a cab.' She shrugged off the concern in his voice. 'It's probably more sensible at this time of night, anyway.'

*   *   *

Cate was glad the weekend was nearly over. On the positive side she had her car back, she thought wryly, packing another load of washing into the machine.

Of Andrew there'd been no sign, and she hadn't had the courage to contact him. She suppressed a sigh. She had no real clue where they stood any more.

He'd shown a marked reluctance to linger when he'd dropped her off last night, merely walking her to the door and leaving her with the cryptic little comment, 'You look done in, Cate. Get some shut-eye.'

She'd had several call-outs during the day but none had required lengthy consultations and at eight o'clock she'd handed over to the agency they used during the week.

Toying with the idea of ringing Andrew, she picked up the phone and immediately put it down. Instead, she went to bed early, falling asleep easily, only to wake a couple of hours later with a terrible feeling of panic in her heart.

Somewhere in her dream she'd lost Andrew, running after him, calling his name. Oh, Lord... Reaching out, she snapped on the bedside lamp and fell back, staring at the ceiling. She felt as though she'd been hit between the eyes.

Shakenly, she faced the truth. She'd fallen head over heels in love with Andrew Whittaker, and it was a deeper, wider emotion than she'd ever imagined.

But what am I going to do, she asked herself bleakly, when all he seems to want is a short-term fling?

With the morning came sanity. It had only been a dream, Cate thought as she flung herself into the shower. She hadn't lost Andrew and there was still time to let things take their course.

I love him, she acknowledged, hugging the secret to herself, and somewhere down the line he'd realise he loved her. He had to. Fate couldn't be that unkind.

There was a definite hint of spring in the air and she dressed accordingly. It felt nice to be out of winter clothes, she reflected, stepping into a swirling skirt with a navy background sprinkled with tiny daisies. With it she teamed a white cotton-knit top and matching lightweight cardigan.

She drove to the surgery, confident that today something positive would happen. Perhaps there'd be a breakthrough with Andrew and he'd tell her he was staying around indefinitely.

'And pigs might fly,' she muttered. Nevertheless, her spirits were still high as she swung out of the Polo and entered the surgery by the rear entrance.

The fragrant smell of coffee took her towards the staffroom.

About to call out a greeting, she stopped outside the partly open door, Chrissie's gasp of disbelief pulling her up short.

'Andrew and Lyn Scali? You must be joking!'

'Saw them with my own eyes.' Jessica's words sent a cold river of dread down Cate's backbone.

'She hit on him all right,' the RN continued. 'Almost as soon as he got back from taking Cate to that house call. He hung around for a few minutes and then they left together.'

Cate didn't wait to hear any more. Feeling shocked through and through, as though she'd been mortally wounded, she fled back to her consulting room.

CHAPTER NINE

HER heart tripping, Cate entered her room, closed the door and stood against it.

How could Andrew?

She felt sick in her stomach, hurt. Angry with him, angry with herself for allowing the same scenario to repeat itself.

Rick had cheated on her, too. But the circumstances were hardly the same, the logical voice inside her pointed out. You were engaged to Rick. Andrew owes you nothing.

She shook her head, ignoring the tight pain inside her chest. But Andrew had held her, kissed her. Acted as though she were someone special. But obviously not special enough.

Damn you, Andrew Whittaker.

Blinking rapidly to clear her vision, she moved to sit behind her desk and methodically began to open her mail. She swallowed hard. How on earth was she going to get through the day? The week?

She tried to claw back composure, rational thought. If only she'd kept her cool professionalism right from the beginning. If only she hadn't fallen in love with him. If only...

By the end of the week she was beginning to wonder if they were both deliberately keeping out of one another's way. It hadn't been all that difficult to achieve.

Cate's mouth tightened. Obviously, it had helped that he'd been fully occupied, getting to grips with a list of new patients. She glanced at her watch, feeling her insides heave. They had the weekly staff meeting in less than an hour, but at least Jon would be there to provide a buffer.

At the knock on her door she looked up, shrinking back in her chair as the familiar face and shoulders found their way around the opening.

'Andrew...' Cate felt her nerves shred. Surely he wasn't here to tell her what he'd done?

'Got a minute?' He didn't bother returning her greeting, just lunged inside, coming to an abrupt halt in front of her desk. Leaning forward, he placed his hands on the polished surface, curving them over the edge.

'I've a patient with shingles,' he said without preamble. 'I haven't seen a case for a while and I'm somewhat out of touch. I've suggested the usual things. Ice packs to shrink the blood vessels and reduce the heat and irritation. Chucking out the soap and using a non-alkaline cleanser instead.'

Cate swallowed, her gaze on the hands that had so recently caressed her. 'Some claim aloe vera helps,' she said.

A slight smile appeared on Andrew's lips. 'His mother suggested castor oil.'

'Taken orally?' Her eyes widened in disbelief.

'Rubbed on, actually.' His eyes narrowed on her face. 'Surely there's something new on the drugs market?'

Cate caught her bottom lip. 'You could try an antiviral medication.' She scribbled a name and handed him the slip of paper. 'It should provide a buffer against the pain.'

'OK, thanks. I'll write him a script and he can give it a shot.'

Cate nodded, tried to smile and couldn't.

Andrew spun round and left.

'So, Cate, what are your plans for the weekend?' Jon asked. 'Doing something nice?'

They had finished their staff meeting and were gathering up their paraphernalia.

Cate's fingers tightened on her pen. The effort of trying to keep up the appearance of normality in front of Andrew was sapping her control. 'I'm going to the Gold Coast straight after work.' She painted on a bright smile. 'Visiting my mum and step-father.'

Andrew gave her a look from under his brows. 'On what part of the coast do they live?'

'Mermaid Beach.' Cate rattled her notes together. 'Mum runs a small art gallery there.'

'Do you paint?' Jon leaned forward with interest.

'Heavens, no!' She laughed lightly. 'Mum doesn't either. She just has a good eye for what will appeal to the public.'

'I must bring Claire down one day. She's on the lookout for something to brighten up our bedroom.' He grinned. 'Right, then.' Jon became businesslike again. 'Andrew, are you settled in OK? Feel all right about covering the weekend?'

'Absolutely.'

'I'm home all weekend if you get into any strife.'

Andrew raised an eyebrow. 'I should be fine. But thanks anyway.'

'Don't fancy a game of squash, I suppose?' Jon looked hopeful. 'One of our regulars has dropped out.'

'Sorry, mate.' Andrew rolled back his shoulders and stretched. 'Much too competitive for me. I prefer a good long run.'

On his own, no doubt. Listening, Cate found she wasn't at all surprised by his choice of exercise.

'What about you, Cate?' Andrew's soft query jerked her back to the present, heightening the terrible tension between them.

She brought her chin up. 'What about me?'

'What do you do for fun and exercise?'

It sounded like a loaded question and she gave him a cool look. 'Whatever pleases me at the time.'

'Well, I'm out of here.' Jon got to his feet, sketching a farewell salute to his contemporaries.

Desperate not to be left alone with Andrew, Cate, too, scrambled out of her chair.

'You don't have to run away on my account, Cate.'

His calm appraisal made her skin warm uncomfortably. 'I have things to do, Dr Whittaker, even if you don't.'

Going to the cooler, she got herself a glass of water and tried to calm down. He looked tired again, she thought. Well, tough! If he was burning the candle at both ends, what could he expect?

'Have a nice weekend, then.' He got to his feet and moved to the door.

'Thanks…' Cate found she couldn't look at him. When the door closed softly she whisked a tissue across her eyes. She wanted to rush after him, plead with him to tell her why things between them had ended like this. Why he preferred Lyn to her.

She had the answer, anyway. Her shoulders slumped tiredly as she made her way back to her room. Lyn was obviously like him, prepared to live life for the moment, whereas, she, Cate could deal only in certainties.

Andrew's flat shrieked of emptiness when he got home. Going through to his bedroom, he undressed, pulling on running shorts and a T-shirt.

He was at some kind of crossroad, he acknowledged silently, stuffing his feet into his trainers. And for perhaps only the second time in his life he didn't know which direction to take.

Stepping outside, he executed a few limbering-up exercises and took the road that would lead him past Cate's place. He didn't know why he felt compelled to do it. She wouldn't be there anyway.

Earlier, when he'd been staring through the window of his surgery, he'd seen her loading an overnight bag into the boot of her car. Right now she'd be on her way to the coast.

The weekend loomed long and lonely in front of him. He blew out a long breath as if to slough off his introspection, hitting his stride and veering off towards the park.

On her arrival at the surgery on Monday morning, Cate passed on the news that Kelly Davenport had delivered a healthy nine-pound daughter on Saturday.

'That's fantastic,' Chrissie beamed. 'Now they have their pigeon pair. When is she bringing the bub in to see us?'

Jessica rolled her eyes. 'Give the girl a chance, ducky. She's probably battling the mild discomfort of stitches and other un-mentionables, after pushing that much baby into the world.'

Cate chuckled, thinking that perhaps Kelly would now be keener than ever for her husband to have a vasectomy.

Hearing the sound of female chatter as he approached the staffroom, Andrew's mouth curved into a dry half-smile. He'd actually looked forward to coming to work this morning, he realised, his own company for most of the weekend having been hardly inspiring. He'd had the chance to sort a few things out in his mind—at least, he hoped so.

'Oh, is that the time?' Chrissie squealed, making a hurried exit.

'I'd better make a move as well.' Jessica rose and pushed her chair in. Her mouth pulled down. 'Seeing it's Monday, I've probably a line of walking wounded waiting to have their various dressings changed. Ah...' She looked up and smiled. 'Here's Andrew come to keep you company, Cate. Catch you both later.'

Politely, Andrew stood aside so that Jessica could make her exit. He brought his head up, catching the guarded expression on Cate's face as she spun round from looking out of the window.

He nodded towards her. 'Cate.'

Her heart took a giant leap. 'Andrew.'

His eyes narrowed on her as she stood there, the lick of want he felt startling him. Slowly, he slid his hands into his back pockets. 'Nice weekend?'

'Lovely. You?'

'No problems.'

Dear heaven, Cate thought in slight desperation, how long could they keep up this kind of soul-destroying, monosyllabic conversation? Their avoidance of one another was eating away at her, affecting her ability to interact naturally with him. Deciding to put an end to it, she plunged into speech. 'I brought back some locally grown tea. It's a fine leaf, rather nice. Would you like a cup?'

A smile edged its way across his mouth. 'Employed you as an ambassador, have they, Cate? I'd love a cup.'

The wave of relief that washed over her was so great she actually managed a full-blown smile, one that reached right into Andrew's heart.

Taking the mug of tea from her out-stretched hand, he said, 'Sit down for a minute, Cate. I want to talk to you.'

For a second she looked at him in alarm, her mind full of awful misgivings. Was it all going to come out now—his reasons for preferring Lyn to her…?

'I had a call from the Salvation Army on the weekend,' he said.

'Oh.' Cate almost reeled from the sense of anticlimax. 'What did they have to say?'

'They had news of Mrs Twigg's daughter. Sadly, she's dead. About a year ago. Unfortunate result of a road accident.'

Cate bit her lip. 'That's bound to be upsetting for Madeleine.'

'There's more.' Andrew's hands spanned his tea-mug. 'There's a granddaughter, Tania Eastley, late twenties, married. Fairly stable, from what the Army could define. Apparently, she's expressed interest in becoming reacquainted with her grandmother.'

Cate nodded slowly. 'That has to be good, doesn't it?'

'One can only hope so.' Andrew raised a dark eyebrow. 'It seems Tania was just a child when the family split happened and her mother never discussed it. For lots of reasons she'd assumed her grandmother was dead.'

Cate swallowed. 'It could all get pretty emotional, couldn't it?'

'Mmm. When are you seeing Madeleine again?'

'Some time during the week.' Cate raised her eyes in query. 'Where does the granddaughter live? Did they tell you?'

'Not all that far from the city, apparently.'

'So it's quite possible Tania could visit Madeleine reasonably often.'

'Well, yes.' Andrew's mouth compressed slightly. 'If Madeleine wants it. Don't get your hopes too high, Cate,' he warned. 'Mrs Twigg might say to hell with the lot of them.'

'I'm sure she wouldn't react like that.' Cate smiled guardedly. 'But I take your point. I'll gauge Madeleine's general well-being when I see her and talk to the registrar. If the consensus is that she's up to hearing this kind of news, I'll let you know and you can pass it along to the Army.'

Andrew frowned down at his tea. 'That's more or less what I told them you'd want to do.'

'Andrew...' Her throat caught. 'Thank you.'

'Hey, I'm merely the messenger.' Impulsively, he reached out and placed his hand on hers.

Suddenly the atmosphere between them was electric.

Cate's body felt as if it were on fire, her heartbeats tripping, gathering speed at a sickening rate. For a long moment they sat there, unmoving, each waiting for the other to break the silence.

Feeling as though her heart were going to burst, Cate slowly withdrew her hand. 'We both have patients waiting,' she said.

Cate was infinitely glad her week had been busy. So busy that she'd had time only to greet Andrew in passing as they'd crossed one another's paths in the normal course of their working days.

The nights had been a different matter entirely. She'd waited for him to make a move to contact her but he hadn't and, despite the relaxation of the tension between them, she wondered if she had any future with him at all.

Harbouring these rather bleak thoughts, she went along to their usual Friday staff meeting.

'What's the latest on your Mrs Twigg, Cate?' Jon asked, settling himself comfortably.

'Perked up like you wouldn't believe. Seems she's quite enjoyed being cosseted. She's all for the retirement home idea now.' Cate cast a wry look at her male contemporaries. 'Actually asked me if I thought she could still get a place. Which she can, of course. I phoned the manager at Jasmine Lodge just a short time ago.'

'A large part of your problem solved, then.' Andrew sent her an encouraging smile.

'I also had a chat to the reg, Catherine Yeo.' Cate met Andrew's eyes directly. 'She's of the opinion Madeleine is up to receiving news of her long-lost family, but preferably before she leaves hospital.'

Andrew nodded briefly. 'I'll get phoning, then, and let the Sally Army know the situation.'

'You will keep me informed?' Cate's voice was more curt than she'd intended, and Andrew cast her a questioning look.

'Of course,' he said, and went on to discuss the status of one of his own patients.

As the meeting wound up, Jon cleared his throat, asking sheepishly, 'Could either of you cover for me for a couple of hours tomorrow?' He turned his palms up expressively. 'I wouldn't ask except Claire's got her mum visiting from the country and she's booked tickets for a theatre matinée for them. I'll have to keep an eye on Mitch.'

'I don't mind.' Cate shrugged. 'What do you want me to do?'

'Provide a medical presence at the grand final of a school rugby tournament. It's between the local grammar school and that trendy new college on the way to the coast.'

'Radleigh,' Cate supplied. 'Have they asked especially for a doctor to be there? I know there's usually an ambulance present at those big games. They can get pretty rough.'

Jon grimaced. 'Seventeen- and eighteen-year-old males hammering the hell out of each other—I should say so. And the business of having medical cover is a personal arrangement between Peter and the headmaster at the grammar school.'

Andrew chuckled. 'Another of Pete's golfing buddies, no doubt.' He ran a hand thoughtfully around his jaw. 'I wouldn't mind watching a game of rugby. Why don't I pick you up, Cate? We'll go together.'

'That's a great idea.' Jon beamed with satisfaction. 'Thanks, guys. I owe you one.'

'I—' Cate opened her mouth and closed it abruptly. Somewhere along the line she'd been totally outmanoeuvred.

It was the next afternoon at the school's wide expanse of playing fields but, despite the balmy sunshine, the clumps of riotously flowering red bottlebrush, the excitement of a grand final, Cate felt twitchy. This whole scene was bringing back memories she would rather not have had.

Taking a deep breath, she looked around her, almost flinching at the over-abundance of male testosterone. She was standing beside Andrew on the sideline of the sports oval next to the first-aid tent.

'I don't know how I let myself be talked into this,' she said pithily.

'You didn't have to come, Cate, you volunteered.'

She frowned. Had she imagined it, or was there a tightness in his voice? She couldn't tell him that she'd been grateful for any opportunity to spend time with him away from the surgery.

'I expect I'll survive,' she said, forcing a smile.

'If it's all too macho for you, you could always go and sit in the car.' Andrew's eyes glinted with dry humour. 'I'll manage.'

'And be accused of being a wimp?' Cate wrapped her arms around her midriff. 'No way. There just seems so many of them.' She shook her head, almost flinching at the sight of the super-fit young males, running on the spot, windmilling their arms and practising packing down with accompanying grunts and growls.

'They're so big!' Cate stepped back quickly, as a kicked ball came threateningly close. 'Like a herd of buffalo—'

'And that's just the home team.' Andrew grinned, amused by her reaction. 'Ah!' He indicated the coach grinding to a stop quite close to them. 'That looks like the visitors arriving now.'

Oh, Lord, more of them. Cate's look was resigned as she watched the rugby team from Radleigh College tumble out of the bus. They were high on adrenalin, at fever pitch with grand final nerves, as they playfully pushed and shoved one another.

The master who had alighted last raised his voice, pointing them in the general direction of the change rooms. Then with a lithe movement he turned as if to view the playing field. And jerked into sudden stillness. 'Cate?' It was an explosion of disbelief.

Cate froze, her arms about her midriff exerting so much pressure she could hardly breathe. He hadn't changed at all. Her mouth tightened. He was still drop-dead handsome, flamboyantly togged out in designer track pants and trainers, a navy and green school-monogrammed sweatshirt defining the hard group of muscles beneath. 'Hello, Rick.'

'What are you doing here?' His voice held an edge of sarcasm. 'You hate rugby.'

Nettled, Cate brought her chin up. 'The same as you, I expect, Rick. I'm working. My colleague and I have been retained by the grammar school to provide medical cover for the game today.'

Her heart thrumming, Cate half turned her head. 'This is Dr Andrew Whittaker. Andrew, Rick De Lisle.'

'Cate's former fiancé,' Rick supplied, as if establishing his status.

Andrew's handshake was brief. 'What's your real job, Mr De Lisle?' he asked, sounding faintly bored.

'I'm the sports master at Radleigh,' Rick blustered. 'Like Cate obviously has, I've changed jobs. Where are you working now?' His green eyes narrowed on her in conjecture.

For a moment Cate considered telling him to mind his own business. But why let him see he'd got to her? He couldn't hurt her any more, though, and that thought helped her to say evenly, 'Ferndale Practice on the south side. How long since you left the university?' she shot back at him.

'A few months.' He lifted a shoulder defensively. 'I much prefer what I'm doing now.'

So tell someone who gives a damn! Cate felt the tight knot of anger in her chest.

Andrew sent her a concerned look. 'We should have a word with the ambulance people, Cate.'

Silently, she blessed his perception, his words giving her the opportunity to escape. 'Have a good game, Rick,' she said shortly, and turned to follow Andrew.

Rick's hand on her arm detained her. 'I'm missing some of my gear,' he said smoothly. 'My track shoes, wetsuit, sundry other stuff. Would you know where I could locate it?'

Cate flung his arm away, as if a venomous snake had settled on her. 'I'd assume someone is probably wearing it,' she said coolly. 'I donated your stuff to Lifeline.'

'You did what?'

Staring at the sulky anger in his face, Cate gathered her strength about her. What on earth had she ever seen in him? She swallowed hard. 'You knew perfectly well your stuff was at my place, Rick. You left it there when I chucked you out—and never bothered to collect it. It's only what you deserved!'

'So high and mighty, Cate,' he sneered. 'So squeaky clean! If you'd lifted your own performance even occasionally, I wouldn't have had to play away from home—'

'Watch your mouth, De Lisle!' Andrew cut in, his eyes burning like blue flames. For two pins he'd have flattened the cretin. Anger, like a loaded spring, coiled in his chest.

'Andrew...' Cate's little cry was anguished. 'Leave it—please. He's not worth it.'

Lord, she was plucky. Andrew shook his head in admiration. A lesser person would have left the scene. But not his Cate. She'd mucked in like a real trouper.

After the first five minutes Andrew had seen it was something of a grudge match between the two teams. And they'd been kept busy.

'It's worse than a bloody war,' he muttered to Cate, as he applied yet another ice pack to an injured player.

'This young man will need stitches.' Beside him, Cate examined a youth with a split above his eye. She signalled the grammar school's coach and explained the medical situation.

'We've an infirmary, Doc. Could you fix him up there?'

'Get him to the local casualty department,' Andrew cut in authoritatively. 'I need Dr Clifford here.'

Now and again Cate paused for breath, noting that Rick had taken himself off to the other side of the rugby pitch. She gave a sigh of relief. If she ever had to speak to him again, it would be too soon.

Finally the match was over and Cate and Andrew were heading down the driveway to the road.

'Remind me to be otherwise engaged around grand final time next year, will you?'

'You didn't enjoy the game?' Cate was somewhat surprised.

'Not much.' His mouth pulled down at the corners. 'It's so professionally orientated now. Some of those kids will be hoping to make a career out of their sport. When I was at school we played for the love of the game, the honour of the school.'

'Nothing stays the same, Andrew,' Cate said quietly.

'Want to talk about it?' He found her hand and held it for a minute.

'No.' Her mind was a mass of jumbled thoughts, feelings and emotions. She laughed. 'Nothing against the Radleigh team, but I'm glad the grammar won.'

Andrew's brief look was razor-sharp. 'I can understand that.' He sensed her instant withdrawal, knew he'd have to tread very lightly if he was to have any chance at all with her.

CHAPTER TEN

'Do you have plans for this evening?' Andrew asked, as he brought the Audi to a stop outside Cate's apartment.

Cate blinked, dragging her thoughts back to the present. 'Plans?' she asked blankly.

'Five-letter word beginning with P.' A wry grin crept across his face.

'No.' She bit her lip. 'I was just going to—'

'Wash your hair?' He raised a dark brow. 'Come round about seven. I'll cook. No pressure, Cate.' His knuckles trailed gently over her cheek. 'We don't have to talk if you don't want to. Just be.'

She looked at him, at the blue eyes searching her face, the broad, intelligent brow furrowed slightly in concern. Her shoulders twitched in a little shrug. 'You don't have to feel sorry for me, Andrew. I know I'm well rid of Rick. And I hadn't thought about him in ages.' Not since I met you, she added silently.

Andrew's mouth drew in. 'I've met men like him. Full of bull and their own importance.'

Cate gave a strained laugh. 'That pretty much describes him. Oh, in the beginning he was attentive, fun to be with. But later I began to suspect he wanted me on his arm like some kind of trophy.'

'The fact you were a doctor probably did his ego a whole heap of good,' Andrew said darkly.

'I suppose…' Cate looked down at her hands. 'As soon as he moved in with me, I began to have serious doubts. I hadn't had much experience with men. I'd had no father figure as I grew up and I went to an all-girls school. Rick just kind of happened, I suppose.' She gave a dry laugh. 'Mum never liked him.'

Andrew reached for her, folding her into a wordless hug, his hand smoothing her hair. 'It might sound old-fashioned, Cate, but he wasn't worthy of you.'

Cate's shoulders lifted as she gave a long sigh. 'He lied, you see. And you can't have a relationship based on lies, can you?'

'No...'

She felt his lips press against her temple, as if she were a child whose hurt had to be soothed. The action was oddly strengthening, warming her through and through. Andrew. She slid her arms around him and hung on.

'Oh, Catie,' he said softly, and then his lips found hers.

Cate's response was electric, desire, sharp and shocking, rocketing through her. She was powerless to end it, to pull away.

Instead, she reached up, locking her arms around his neck, weaving her fingers through the soft tufts of hair at his nape. She made a little sound in her throat as he lifted her closer, his hand, warm and gentle, cupping her breast.

'You feel so good,' he murmured into her throat, the tip of his tongue teasing the soft little hollow. 'Sweet Cate,' he sighed, resting his cheek against her hair and holding her as if he'd never let her go.

How long they stayed like that Cate didn't know or care. She only knew it felt absolutely and completely right. No words were necessary. I love this man. The words echoed over and over in her head and she snuggled even closer.

When he at last lifted his head, she made a small questioning murmur. 'What?'

'The sun's almost set,' he said. 'It'll be dark in a few minutes.'

'Mmm.' Cate raised her gaze, watching the last lingering colour begin to leach from the pale canopy of sky.

'We'd better make a move.' Andrew pulled slowly back, then unexpectedly dipped his head and pressed his mouth to hers. As a kiss it was fleeting yet oddly fierce. 'Come home with me now, Cate. We'll detour and get some wine.'

What could she say? Right at that moment she wanted to be with him more than anything else in the world. And if he thought himself only capable of offering her a short-term relationship, well, so be it. She'd face the end of the affair when she had to. Meanwhile, she needed Andrew as much as she needed her own breathing.

'I've found a reasonable cellar off Macklin Street,' he said, pulling away from the kerb and heading back towards the main road. He caught her hand and turned it palm up, kissing it. 'What do you fancy?'

You. Cate's heart thumped. 'As in wine?'

'Mmm.' He gave her back her hand. 'Red or white?'

'I don't mind, really.'

He laughed, a small, satisfied sound. 'We'll get both, then.'

Cate rolled her eyes. 'You make it sound like we'll be up all night, drinking.'

'Perhaps we will.' The words were softly spoken, throaty. 'But not necessarily drinking.'

The atmosphere between them was suddenly throbbing with expectation. Cate took a shallow breath, crossing her arms against her chest, every nerve ending tightening with the wash of emotion pouring through her.

'Hell's teeth!'

Andrew's explosion of alarm had Cate snapping back to the present and jerking forward to peer through the windscreen.

'Oh, my God...' she whispered, registering what Andrew had already seen—the small car in front of them, travelling too fast, had failed to negotiate a corner and side-swiped a power pole. With a feeling of disbelief, Cate watched the car lurch off the road, stopping with a sickening thump.

Swearing under his breath, Andrew ground the Audi to a halt. 'Emergency services, Cate!' Tossing her his mobile phone, he threw himself out of the car and began running towards the accident scene.

Forcing herself to keep steady, Cate dialled the number that would link the three services. It was an age since she'd attended a road accident, but suddenly, miraculously, her reaction in emergencies became automatic, her medical training overcoming her nerves.

Andrew had left his keys in the ignition and she yanked them out, running to unlock the boot of his car.

Cate grabbed everything she could lay her hands on, blessing the fact that Andrew was such a methodical man. He'd obviously taken extra precautions, knowing they would be covering the rugby game.

There was even a small fire extinguisher which Cate tucked under her arm, adding to her burden of medical gear as she ran towards the partially crumpled small car.

Please, she implored silently. Don't let it be fatal...

To Cate, the next minutes became surreal. As she reached the car there was a snap like the crack of a whip and the car's bonnet burst into flames.

'Give me that!' Grabbing the fire extinguisher, Andrew pulled the pin and, holding the small unit upright, began to sweep the quelling agent from side to side.

'I got the driver out,' he yelled to Cate. 'But there's a woman in there. She's pregnant.'

Oh, dear God. Dropping her gear, Cate ran to the passenger side of the car. One glance told her the door had taken the force of the impact and was jammed shut.

'*Andrew!*' Cate screamed. Inside the car the trapped woman was making frantic signs, tears streaming down her face. 'I can't get the door open.'

'Let me try.' He pushed Cate roughly aside. 'Damn it to hell,' he grated. 'Where's the cavalry when you need them?'

Cate looked frantically around. There wasn't a chance of help from a local source either. The accident had happened in an industrial area with business premises closed for the weekend.

Andrew swore, his shoulders straining as he tried to release the door. 'This design should be bloody well banned from the roads,' he snarled through gritted teeth, thumping the metal with the heel of his hand. 'This isn't going to work.'

'What about car tools?' Cate's head spun back to the Audi. 'Do you have something?'

'Tyre lever—' Andrew was running.

Cate was beginning to feel totally impotent. Darkness had fallen and the street lighting was next to useless. Leaning forward, she cupped her hands around her eyes and peered into the rear of the car. What she saw there made her gasp, set up a whole new chain of urgency.

Andrew was back and within seconds the door was wrenched open.

'My baby…' The woman's voice faded to a whisper. 'Get him out—please.'

'It'll be OK.' Andrew's voice and actions were gentle as he lifted the woman out and laid her on the blanket Cate had quickly thrown on the grassy verge. 'We're doctors. We'll get your baby out.'

'Andrew.' Cate's voice shook. 'I think she means her other child. There's a toddler strapped in the back seat.'

'And that car could blow any minute.' His voice was tight with strain. 'Right. I'll try and lever the driver's seat forward and we'll get the child out that way. You'll have to do it, Cate. You're smaller.'

Cate realised she'd reached a new plateau of calm, enabling her mind to become sharp and practical. 'I can do that,' she said, and promptly did.

The toddler seemed unhurt but Cate guessed he was quite shocked. 'Come on, baby,' she crooned, releasing the harness and lifting him. His little arms clasped her neck and she backed slowly out of the battered car.

'Well done,' Andrew said gravely, taking the child and wrapping him in one of the space blankets. 'Let's put you over here,' he said, 'where your mum can see you.'

'How's the driver?' Cate began to unpack a first-aid kit.

'Still out of it.' Andrew grabbed a torch from the emergency pack. 'Nothing broken.'

'How long since you've delivered a baby?' Cate asked. The woman was keening softly, pulling her knees up as though she wanted to push.

'Not as long as you might think, Dr Clifford.' There was a lightness in Andrew's voice. 'And I can tell you this little person isn't waiting for any ambulance.'

Between gasps, the woman told them her name was Anna Ross. 'We were on our way to the hospital. How is…my husband? Did you say you're doctors?' The questions bubbled out.

'Yes, we're doctors.' Cate angled the torch so Andrew could check how far their patient was dilated. 'I'm Cate and this is Andrew. Your husband has been knocked out but he doesn't seem to have anything broken.'

'The head's crowning,' Andrew said. 'You can start to push, Anna. But gently, OK?'

The emergency vehicles arrived one after the other.

'Perfect timing,' Andrew grunted. 'Now we've done all the hard stuff.'

Cate smiled. In reality it had been only minutes but she could quite see Andrew's point. It had felt like hours until they'd got

Anna and her little boy free from the car. She could hear Andrew quietly encouraging the mother and realised she'd seen yet another side of him.

'Sterile dressings, Cate,' he snapped. 'Can you unwrap them, please? And then help Anna into position.'

Cate moved quickly.

The infant, a boy, was born under torchlight a few minutes later. 'He's a beauty.' Andrew's face was rapt as he cut the cord and handed him across to his mother.

'We'll take over now, Doc.'

'They're all yours, folks.' Andrew caught Cate's hand and stood back as the paramedics knelt by the new mother and baby, preparing them to be lifted onto the waiting stretcher.

'Where were you booked to have your baby, Anna?' Cate lifted the toddler and held him to her.

'St Anne's.' Anna managed a shaky smile. 'Thank you both—so much. Is

Keith—?' She looked anxiously to where her husband was lying.

'I'm about to check him over now.' Andrew reached out, stroking the baby's plump little cheek with a long, blunt finger. 'I'm sure he'll be fine.'

'Are you?' Cate asked quietly, as she handed Andrew his medical case.

'Reasonably.' Andrew made his examination thoroughly. 'Pupils equal and reacting,' he said. 'So far so good. Mr Ross, can you hear me?'

The man groaned, his eyes flickering.

'Your family's OK.'

Suddenly Keith Ross's eyes flew wide open. 'Baby—' he gasped.

'You have a new son.' Andrew was monitoring the man's pulse.

'Do you remember the car crash, Keith?' Cate tucked the space blanket more firmly around him.

'Yes—too fast. Brakes jammed. Hell...'

'This one for us, Doc?' One of the paramedics joined the group.

'Please.' Andrew gave his findings quickly, 'BP one-forty over eighty. Pulse ninety-five.'

'And could you try to get Mr Ross into the same hospital as his wife, please?' Cate asked.

'Shouldn't be a problem, Doc. Lucky you were so quick on the scene, from all accounts.'

Within a few minutes the Ross family were on their way to hospital. The police team was taking measurements for the accident report and the fire officers had ensured the car was now safe to be towed away.

Silently, as both were preoccupied, Cate and Andrew loaded their gear back into the Audi.

'Don't forget this.' Cate handed over the fire extinguisher. 'I hope there'll be grandparents or someone who'll be able to look after the toddler until his parents are out of hospital,' she said.

'The staff at St Anne's will sort that out.' Andrew stowed the extinguisher in a corner of the boot. 'But whatever, I'm sure you'll want to check on them yourself in the next day or two. Or you wouldn't be the Cate I know.' He hooked an arm around her shoulders and hugged her to his side.

At the passenger side of the car he turned, drawing her gently into his arms, locking his fingers over the small of her back and easing her up against him. 'Are we still on for tonight?' he asked huskily.

'I hope so.' Cate wound her arms around his neck. 'But could you drop me home first? I need to shower and change after this lot.'

'Ditto. And we still have to get the wine.'

Cate rang the bell on Andrew's front door. The nerves in her stomach were jangling.

Well, why wouldn't she be anxious? She made a tiny sound. She had no great experience with men. What if she was hopeless, turned him off?

Wrapping her arms tightly around her midriff, she waited for him to answer the door.

'Hello.' He opened the door with a flourish and all her doubts dissolved like snowflakes in the sun. It was Andrew, the man she loved, big and rugged, dressed in battered jeans and a white T-shirt. In contrast to her, he seemed utterly relaxed.

'Not too early, am I?' Cate felt his hand warmly on the small of her back as he ushered her inside. He smelled of soap and water, his hair still damp from the shower.

'Not a bit. I've even got a start on our dinner.'

'Are we having the famous risotto?'

'You bet. Glass of wine?'

'Please. Oh.' She bit her lip. 'I didn't bring anything towards the meal.'

'Cate...' His reprimand was soft. 'You didn't have to bring anything. I invited you, remember?'

She swallowed the sudden lump in her throat. How could she have forgotten? While he got the wine, she took a cursory look around. Was she subconsciously looking for traces that Lyn Scali had been here? she fretted. And if she found any, what then? Accepting the glass of white wine from his outstretched hand, she began to sip it slowly.

'The plant looks all right,' she observed lightly, and saw him grin.

'We have amazing conversations.'

Cate wrinkled her nose at him, moving to sit on one of the high stools. Her head on one side, she watched him, his movements easy, casual, confident as he stirred the rice.

The wine began to form a warm glow inside her and almost automatically her gaze drifted over Andrew Whittaker, the man. Half closing her eyes, she absorbed his essence, letting her senses run rife.

Her fingers uncurled from around her glass as if they had a mind of their own, their mission to strip off his T-shirt and stroke the tight cord of muscles beneath.

She took another mouthful of wine, observing he probably hadn't had a haircut since he'd been discharged from the army. The dark strands were now longer, softly touching the base of his neck.

'Chicken stock...' came the preoccupied self-directed instruction as he opened the pantry and peered inside.

'Right in front of you.' Cate couldn't hide her chuckle.

'Smart alec.' He looked back over his shoulder at her and grinned.

'What happens now?' she asked, her interest in culinary things sharpening as he ripped open the carton of prepared stock and began to dribble it into the rice mixture.

'I have to trickle this in until the rice comes to the right consistency. It takes about fifteen minutes.' He sent her a dry look. 'Hope you're not starving, Doctor?'

'I am, actually.' Cate was feeling pleasantly relaxed from the wine. 'Nothing except a sandwich at lunch.'

Andrew clicked his tongue, aiming his wooden spoon at her in playful admonishment. 'Be careful the wine doesn't knock you over, then.'

She giggled. 'I think it already has. Want me to set the table?'

'Ah…' He looked baffled. 'That might be a bit difficult.'

Cate shook her head in resignation. 'You still don't have one, do you?' She slid off the stool. 'I guess we could have a picnic, then.' She'd noticed some big floor cushions in the lounge room as she'd come in. And an ancient sea captain's chest which would serve as an impromptu table.

'Sounds good to me.' He began to toss onion and garlic in another pan. 'There's a boxful of stuff Ellie gave me over there in the corner. You might find something useful.'

Cate rolled her eyes, wondering what he'd deem 'useful', but, in fact, she did find long white candles which she lit and placed at each end of the seachest. The soft light lent quite a romantic ambience to the room, she decided, plumping up the cushions. Sifting through his collection of compact discs, she found something which would pass for mood music and slid it into the player.

Andrew hadn't missed a beat of her studied little preparations. Almost angrily, he threw a handful of spinach leaves into the pan. Why didn't he just tell her and to hell with the consequences?

'That was simply wonderful.'

Andrew's look was indulgent as he

watched her fork up the last morsel. 'Well, go on, then,' he coaxed. 'Aren't you going to ask me for the recipe?'

'I'd assumed you'd be a gentleman and tell me,' she countered drily, dipping into the salad bowl for a leaf of frilly lettuce to cleanse her palate.

'Let's have some more music.' He got to his feet and ambled across to the CD player. In a few seconds the haunting sounds of the Uilleann pipes of Ireland filled the room, steeping them in a magical world that held only the two of them.

Snuggled against the warm bulk of Andrew's chest, Cate lost track of time, wishing only that they could stay like this for ever.

The candles had almost burned down when they finally stirred. 'Come on.' Cate nudged him with her elbow. 'Let's get this lot washed up before it's too sticky to cope with.'

'Ever-practical Cate.' Andrew smudged a kiss across her temple. 'Just don't mention dishwashers,' he warned.

Stacking plates deftly, she gave him a pained look. 'Would I?'

He chuckled, watching her walk from the room. God, it felt good to have her here. He waited a minute and then hauled himself from the cushions, padding after her to the kitchen. He saw she'd already filled the sink with suds.

Cate threw him a look over her shoulder. 'Coffee shouldn't be long.'

'Good.' He wrapped his arms around her from behind.

Half turning, she said almost shyly, 'It was nice, having someone cook for me.'

'You're very welcome, Cate.'

'Andrew!' She flicked soap bubbles at him, squirming with laughter as he nuzzled the side of her throat. 'Are you going to help or not?'

'Or not.' He turned her into his arms. 'Let them soak. I'll do them tomorrow.' He speared her with a brilliant blue gaze. 'I'd much rather do this…'

She made a tiny inarticulate sound as his lips found hers, their touch light, delicate, searching, before he gathered her in.

Cate wound her arms around him, revelling in the muscled contours of his back, the ridges that flexed beneath her palms. A tide of need overcame her, shocking in its intensity.

'I want to make love to you…'

Cate gasped, feeling his matching urgency as he flicked open her shirt, bending to put his mouth to the hollow between her breasts, peeling back the edges of her camisole, tracing each tiny exposure of skin with his tongue.

Reeling, she felt filled with a life-giving force, wanting him more than she'd ever wanted anything in her life. He hadn't said he loved her. He'd offered no future together. But that was as straws in the wind compared with what she could have with him now. Tomorrow was for tomorrow.

'Cate?' He said her name with a rich huskiness that rippled along her skin.

'Yes,' she breathed, hearing her own heartbeat, already feeling the imprint of him on her body.

At the door of his bedroom she faltered, her eyes taking in the softly lit space, one bedside lamp giving out a gentle beam across the pillow.

'Cate? What is it?'

His voice was throaty, deep inside her head, and she swallowed, overcome with nerves. She turned to him, her fingers clutching the soft stuff of his T-shirt. 'Andrew... What if...?'

'No.' He swung her off her feet, depositing her neatly on the side of the bed. 'No ghosts. Not tonight. This is us. You and me.' He bent, brushing her lips once, and again. 'This will be so special between us

Cate. So special.' He pulled off his shirt and threw it to one side.

Shakily, Cate followed suit, releasing the last of the buttons on her shirt and stepping out of her jeans.

Watching her, Andrew made a dry, deep sound in his throat. 'Women do that so much more gracefully than men.'

'Can't say I've noticed.' Cate gave a strangled laugh.

'You're beautiful, Cate.'

She blushed. 'You would say that.'

'With just one difference, sweetheart.' His laugh was harsh as he caught her, lifting her and placing her with the gentlest movement in the middle of the wide bed. 'I happen to mean it.'

Almost mesmerised, Cate watched as he stripped off the rest of his clothes and came back to lie beside her, his body hard and warm against hers.

The window was partially open, the heady mix of stocks and sweet peas scenting the night air. Spring, she thought. New beginnings. On a little sigh she whispered his name, turning her body towards his.

'Cate…'

At his touch she trembled, awash with love for him. And his hands were gentle, knowing, taking her on a voyage of awakening, of seeking, sculpting her face, her breasts, the curve of her spine. Fire danced in her veins as he leaned against her, his mouth replacing his hands.

'Let me,' she whispered, dazed with emotion, her hands aching to discover him. She heard his groan of pleasure and then they were lost in the taste and texture of one another, moving in perfect rhythm.

When their climax came, Cate thought she had fallen off the edge of the world in a flood-tide of ecstasy the like of which she'd never known.

As her heart steadied, she found Andrew beside her, his hand protectively over her quivering ribcage, his gaze riveted on her face. 'Well, well,' he murmured. 'What do you know?'

Her face crumpled. 'A bit more than I knew yesterday. Oh, Andrew…' Overcome, she turned her face into his shoulder.

'Told you, didn't I?' His tone was softly teasing and he kissed her shoulder, her throat, spreading her hair like silver rain across the pillow.

Cate realised she must have slept because she woke suddenly to find Andrew sitting on the edge of the bed beside her. He was fully dressed. 'Oh, hi.' She struggled to sit up, grasping the sheet to cover herself. 'What time is it?'

'Late. Or early.' He touched a finger to her cheek, moving it to outline her jaw. 'Depends how you want to look at it. Could you get dressed?'

Cate blinked. Was he chucking her out of his bed? It certainly sounded like it. 'I…guess so.'

He nodded and rose to his feet. 'Then I'll run you home.'

She managed a tight smile. 'Worried about your reputation, Doctor?'

'Not at all.' He looked at her blankly.

When they got back to her apartment, Cate unlocked the front door and stood there. A thousand questions were bubbling on her tongue. 'Will I see you tomorrow?' she asked, and saw him frown.

'No, sorry.' He lifted a hand and rubbed the back of his neck. 'The Camerons have invited me out for the day on their yacht.'

'Whoo-whee.' Cate made a face. 'What is it? Small thank you for saving his life?'

Andrew pretended to shudder. 'God forbid!'

Cate drummed up a tight smile. 'Weatherwise, it should be superb. And Moreton Bay is a sailing paradise—'

'Cate.' He took a step forward, folding her in his arms. 'Stop babbling. I wish I could take you along but—'

'Andrew.' She placed her finger across his mouth. 'I understand.'

She just wished she understood why he hadn't wanted to spend the whole night with her.

She was still pondering the question long after he'd gone.

CHAPTER ELEVEN

ANDREW felt bad.

He'd meant to talk to Cate before now. At least phone her. But each time he'd made the decision he'd backtracked. How did you solve the insoluble?

She must have him labelled as some kind of insensitive jerk, he lamented, scrubbing his knuckles along his jaw. He should have left things well alone.

But you had to have it all, Whittaker. Curse your pathetic hide!

By Thursday Cate was going crazy.

She couldn't believe he'd made no effort to see her outside of the surgery, but there had been nothing from him. Nothing to reinforce the fact that, physically, they'd been as close as any two people could have been. They'd become lovers, for heaven's sake!

As she made her way to his consulting room she was left with the stark, miserable conclusion that he'd been merely using her.

Yet somehow, deep within her, she couldn't believe that. Wouldn't.

Her heart thumping, she knocked on his door and popped her head in. 'Hello.' She had difficulty in getting the word past her throat. 'Chrissie said you were between patients.'

'Cate…' Andrew swung quickly off his chair. Reaching out, he took her hands. 'I was just coming to see you.'

'Were you?' She didn't quite believe him but, oh, dear God, how she wanted to. 'I have news about Madeleine and Tania.' She rushed into speech.

'And?'

'It went well.'

'That's brilliant.' Andrew squeezed her hands. 'Well done, you.'

She gave a cracked laugh. 'Well done, all of us, I think. Tania and her husband are going to be family support for Madeleine, organise her move to Jasmine Lodge and so on.'

Andrew's eyes suddenly narrowed and he guided her into a chair. 'Are you OK about that?'

'Absolutely.' Cate dismissed his concern. 'It's a far better outcome for Madeleine. Having her family around her, even if it's only a tiny part of it, has to beat having no one at all.' She lifted a shoulder. 'And I'll still be her GP even when she moves to her new address.'

Andrew looked thoughtful, propping himself on the edge of the desk next to her. 'What about the Ross family?' He gave her an indulgent half-smile. 'Have you checked on them?'

'Mmm.' Her mouth folded in primly. 'They've all gone home. Oh, and I did learn something else.'

His dark brows quirked. 'Are you going to tell me?'

'They've named the new baby Andrew.'

'Poor kid.' He gave an embarrassed laugh, but Cate could tell he was pleased.

'Are you doing anything this evening?' she asked before she could lose her nerve.

'Uh…no. Don't think so.' Straightening, he pushed himself upright. 'Would you like to go out for a meal, perhaps?'

'No, I'll feed you. The evenings are so mild at the moment I thought we could barbecue a couple of steaks.'

'The same ones we never got round to eating?'

'Please.' Cate rolled her eyes theatrically. 'They're long gone. No, I've some excellent T-bones from Trev.'

'Should I ask?' Andrew wanted to carry on the absurd conversation just to keep her with him for a few seconds more.

Her mouth tilted. 'Trevor James, my patient who's a butcher.'

'Ah!' Andrew snapped his fingers. 'Got you. We exchanged small talk over his X-rays.'

About a hundred years ago. The chair rocked slightly as Cate got to her feet. 'See you about seven, then.'

'Cate...' Andrew let out his breath on a harsh sigh. 'I can't forget how we were together. How right it felt.'

So right he'd made no effort to refer to it, let alone touch her, for almost a week! She opened her mouth and closed it, the words she'd been about to deliver jamming at the look on his face. The naked vulnerability that turned her inside out.

Oh, Andrew.

She shot out of the door before he could do or say anything more that would place her even further under his spell.

As soon as Cate arrived home from the surgery, she went outside to her little courtyard. She had a portable barbecue that took a while to prepare for cooking. Placing the special heat beads under the metal grid, she lit them and left them to do their job.

Excitement was pouring through her as she ran upstairs. She showered and shampooed her hair, blow-drying it until it fell in soft, loose curls around her shoulders.

What should she wear? Uncertainty gripped her and then she took a deep breath, deciding to please herself.

Her underwear was hardly seduction material, she thought wryly, but it was pretty and new in soft white cotton sprinkled with rosebuds.

For the outer layer she chose a red summery skirt slashed at the side seam and a silky sleeveless T-shirt that exactly matched the red in the skirt.

Swiping on a bright matt lipstick, she took a deep breath, willing her heart to stop its crazy dance against her ribs.

'You look good enough to eat,' Andrew quipped when she let him in.

Cate gave a choked laugh. 'That could be awkward. I've just put the steaks on.'

'Oh, good.' He followed her through to the kitchen. 'I could eat a horse.'

'Damn.' Cate clicked her tongue. 'I knew I should've stopped by the pony club for something.'

'Sharp, this evening, aren't we, Doctor?' He lifted a hand, touching the back of her head in the lightest caress. 'I've brought some lager.'

Cate gave a breathless laugh. 'Sounds just right. Glasses in the top cupboard. I'm throwing a green salad together.'

They sat on in the courtyard long after they'd finished eating. They talked about everything under the sun except, Cate realised, the subject uppermost in their minds.

Is he going to leave? she wondered, stacking the dishwasher with slow deliberation. Or is he going to ask to stay?

She didn't have long to wait to find out.

'That's all squared away,' he said, coming in from the courtyard and closing the sliding door.

'Thanks.' Cate twiddled with the dish-washer to set it off on its cycle.

'Cate…' Andrew's arms wrapped around her from behind, his voice throaty as he asked, 'Have you changed your mind about us?'

Just tell him you're totally confused about where you stand with him, a little inner voice whispered. But how could she put him on the spot? He hadn't promised anything. Not really.

'N-no.' Her voice wavered and then firmed enough for her to say, 'I haven't changed, Andrew.'

She turned into his arms and he hugged her tightly. Without further words, they walked upstairs.

Their love-making was passionate. Cate wanted him desperately, becoming more daring than she had believed possible. Their final coming together was shatteringly sweet, leaving them exhausted against one another.

When the tumult within them had stilled, Andrew scooped her up, covering her with tiny, loving kisses that to Cate, at least, conveyed more than words ever could.

She fell asleep in his arms.

Andrew's cry woke her, strident, echoing around the walls of the room.

Cate jerked upright. Her heart pounding, she snapped on the bedside lamp. 'Andrew,' she whispered in alarm. He was tangled in the bedclothes, between sleep and wakefulness, caught in the grip of some awful nightmare.

His muffled pleas of desperation tore at Cate's heart. 'Andrew,' she urged softly. 'Hush, it's OK—it's OK.' His moan became a shuddering breath.

'It's all right, sweetheart.' Cate bent towards him, cradling his dark head against her, murmuring reassurances over and over.

Finally he went still and she sensed he'd woken. It was a long time until he moved.

His eyes flicked open and he looked at her. 'Oh, hell, Cate.' He shook his head, squeezing his eyes shut as if in pain. 'Some kind of hero, aren't I?' he said bitterly.

Cate's arms tightened about him as it all fell into place. The man she loved was suffering from PTSD—post-traumatic stress disorder.

Heaven knew when he'd last had a proper night's sleep. That he'd tried his darnedest to hide it was obvious, even going to the extent of turfing her out the other night.

'You poor love,' she murmured, working her fingers into the muscles of his neck and shoulders. It seemed an age until she felt him relax.

'It's almost daylight,' she said close to his ear. 'Why don't you have a shower and I'll make some tea? Then we'll talk.'

'Ever the little fixer, aren't you, Cate?' he said in a cold, quiet voice. 'Talking won't help.'

'For heaven's sake, Andrew!' Thrusting herself out of bed, she reached for her gown. 'Talking to the right people will help. Have you actually had any counselling since you left the army?'

His silence told her everything she needed to know. 'I'm using the main bathroom,' she said, flipping out fresh underclothes from her drawer. 'Use the *en suite*. I'll see you in the kitchen in ten minutes.'

CHAPTER TWELVE

CATE gave a fractured sigh.

Had she come on too strongly? Probably. But, then, doctors for the most part were slow off the mark when it came to their own health and well-being.

Wrapping her arms around her, she peered through the kitchen window, noticing the pink glow in the sky already heralding sunrise. She turned as Andrew came in. He'd obviously showered and dressed. 'Hi.' She sent him a guarded smile.

'Hi.' He let his breath out in a harsh sigh. 'Sorry if I seemed to snarl at you earlier.'

Cate twitched a shrug of dismissal, watching him pull out a chair and sit at the pine table. She busied herself pouring tea and then set the blue teapot between them on the table, recalling her mother's little gem of wisdom that many a knotty problem had been solved over a pot of tea. 'Would you like some toast to go with this?' she asked.

'No, thanks. Tea's just what I need.'

For a few awful seconds they sat there. Cate's heart was pounding, uncertainty spreading to every part of her body. Just when she had decided to initiate the conversation, Andrew burst into speech.

'Um...I don't know where to start.' He looked down into the dark brew in his mug.

'Perhaps you could start by answering my earlier question,' she said carefully. 'Have you had any counselling since you left the army?'

He shook his head. 'I thought I could handle things myself. Clearly, I haven't succeeded.'

Well, at least he was now admitting he needed help. Cate crossed her fingers. That had to be a giant step forward. 'Would you like a referral to someone?' she asked.

'No, but thanks. There are avenues I can and will follow up. Specialist counselling. I know what I have to do, what I ought to have done weeks ago.' He took a large swallow of his tea and put his mug down, spanning his fingers around it.

'The children's plight was the worst.' As if the safety valve had at last been released, he began to open up. 'Now, with hindsight, I see that's what finally got to me.' He brushed a hand across his eyes, symbolically erasing the images.

'They were so stoic, Cate. Like wise old people. There was a nine-year-old girl whose parents had been killed in the tidal wave. She'd assumed care of her two younger siblings as a matter of course. And there were so many crushed little limbs, amputations done on the trot. And people who came to the field hospital with nothing more than bits of cardboard holding bones together—if they were lucky.'

'Andrew.' Cate's head went back and she looked at him. 'It might sound trite but you could only do what you could. No one can do more than that. Even as a bystander, watching television, I could see it was a tragedy of immense proportions. But for those of you who were there, I can't even begin to imagine how it was, how you coped day after day.'

'I lost my professional objectivity,' he said flatly.

'How could you not?' She leant away from him, staring up into his eyes. They really were the most amazing blue, she thought absently.

After what seemed the longest time, he reached across and took her hands, enfolding them within his. 'I love you, Cate.' His lopsided smile was edged with vulnerability. 'At least I know I've got that right.'

'Oh, Andrew…' Cate felt as though a huge, crippling weight had been lifted from her. Tears sprang to her eyes and she blinked them back. 'I love you, too. I have done for ages.'

He moved then, spinning back his chair. A giant groan erupted from him as he lifted her to her feet and gathered her in, holding her so tightly Cate thought her ribs would crack. But she wasn't about to complain.

'When did you know you loved me?' she asked coyly, as his arms slackened.

He pressed his forehead against hers. 'The morning you brought me that crazy half-tree. When you'd gone, it suddenly hit me like an avalanche.'

'The tree?' Cate snickered.

'No.' He cupped her face and kissed her very slowly and thoroughly. 'I discovered I was in love with you, Cate Clifford. Needed you in my life.' His mouth quirked ruefully. 'But I did my best not to let the reality in. After all, it didn't fit in with what I'd planned, did it?'

'No ties.' She made a small face. 'People change their ideas all the time, Andrew. And it's time you settled down. As long as it's with me,' she emphasised, snuggling closer. 'Andrew?' she asked, after a while.

'Mmm?' He pulled back to look at her.

Cate pouted, running her finger down the front of his shirt. 'Have you seen much of Lyn Scali?'

He looked at her, as if he needed to haul his thoughts back from a million miles away. 'Where did that come from?'

'I—just wondered. Someone said you left the Maguires' farewell party together.'

'Did we?' His brow furrowed. 'Ah, yes. I remember now. Lyn didn't have her car. She was going on night duty. I gave her a lift to the hospital.' He gave a little click of admonishment. 'You thought we'd got off together, didn't you?'

'Well, all the signs were there,' Cate said hotly. 'And Claire was overtly match-making.'

He chuckled. 'Lyn told me. But Claire was wasting her time. Lyn's got some guy in the States, a surgeon attached to one of the care agencies. She's meeting him over there for New Year. Oh, Catie…' He tilted her face, their gazes colliding in a dazzling look of love. 'Marry me,' he said gravely.

'Yes,' she replied simply. 'When the time is right for us.' With the softest look in her eyes, she touched his cheek. 'In the meantime, you could move in with me, couldn't you?'

'Not yet.' He took a deep, shuddering breath and held her close. 'I need to sort myself out first.'

'That won't take long,' she said confidently, and felt his arms tighten.

'I love your place, Cate.'

She heard the smile in his voice. 'Feels like home already, huh?'

'Oh, definitely.' His eyes were full of amusement. 'And also for one other compelling reason. The decorating's all done.'

'But with the summer coming…' Cate laughed softly and stood on tiptoe. 'Perhaps we could rearrange the—'

What she'd been about to say Andrew never discovered. Instead, he bent swiftly and silenced her mouth with his.

MEDICAL ROMANCE™

Large Print

Titles for the next six months...

August

A MOTHER BY NATURE	Caroline Anderson
HEART'S COMMAND	Meredith Webber
A VERY SPECIAL CHILD	Jennifer Taylor
THE ELUSIVE DOCTOR	Abigail Gordon

September

DOCTOR ON LOAN	Marion Lennox
A NURSE IN CRISIS	Lilian Darcy
MEDIC ON APPROVAL	Laura MacDonald
TOUCHED BY ANGELS	Jennifer Taylor

October

RESCUING DR RYAN	Caroline Anderson
FOUND: ONE HUSBAND	Meredith Webber
A WIFE FOR DR CUNNINGHAM	Maggie Kingsley
RELUCTANT PARTNERS	Margaret Barker

MILLS & BOON®

Makes any time special™

MEDICAL ROMANCE™

 *Large Print*

November

CLAIMED: ONE WIFE	Meredith Webber
A NURSE'S FORGIVENESS	Jessica Matthews
THE ITALIAN DOCTOR	Jennifer Taylor
NURSE IN NEED	Alison Roberts

December

COMING HOME TO DANIEL	Josie Metcalfe
DR MATHIESON'S DAUGHTER	Maggie Kingsley
THE NURSE'S DILEMMA	Gill Sanderson
THE HONOURABLE DOCTOR	Carol Wood

January

REDEEMING DR HAMMOND	Meredith Webber
AN ANGEL IN HIS ARMS	Jennifer Taylor
THE PARAMEDIC'S SECRET	Lilian Darcy
THE CONSULTANT'S CONFLICT	Lucy Clark

MILLS & BOON®

Makes any time special™